PRAISE FOR *THE GAUNTLET*

"Jumanji meets Spy Kids in this action-packed story . . .
An exciting, clever debut."
—*Booklist Online*

"Readers who love gaming and adventure will line up to
read this book. . . . This will be a popular addition to the fantasy
adventure genre in any middle level collection."
—*School Library Connection*

PRAISE FOR *THE BATTLE*

"Riazi once again offers a fast-paced story in a changing
game world with floating skyscrapers, flying cars, flavorful food and
sweets, and a giant talking mouse. . . . An exciting return."
—*Kirkus Reviews*

"Fantasy featuring people of color is sorely needed,
and while this adventurous sequel could be read on its
own, it's recommended to buy both novels for kids who
love action-packed science fiction."
—*School Library Journal*

THE
BATTLE

KARUNA RIAZI

SALAAM
READS

New York • London • Toronto • Sydney • New Delhi

An imprint of Simon & Schuster Children's Publishing Division
1230 Avenue of the Americas, New York, New York 10020
This book is a work of fiction. Any references to historical events, real people, or real places are used fictitiously. Other names, characters, places, and events are products of the author's imagination, and any resemblance to actual events or places or persons, living or dead, is entirely coincidental.
Text copyright © 2019 by CAKE Literary LLC
Cover illustrations copyright © 2019 by Mehrdad Isvandi
All rights reserved, including the right of reproduction in whole or in part in any form.
SALAAM READS is a trademark of Simon & Schuster, Inc.
For information about special discounts for bulk purchases, please contact Simon & Schuster Special Sales at 1-866-506-1949 or business@simonandschuster.com.
The Simon & Schuster Speakers Bureau can bring authors to your live event. For more information or to book an event, contact the Simon & Schuster Speakers Bureau at 1-866-248-3049 or visit our website at www.simonspeakers.com.
Also available in a Salaam Reads hardcover edition
Cover design by Krista Vossen
Interior design by Hilary Zarycky
The text for this book was set in Berling.
Manufactured in the United States of America
0720 OFF
First Salaam Reads paperback edition August 2020
2 4 6 8 10 9 7 5 3 1
The Library of Congress has cataloged the hardcover edition as follows:
Names: Riazi, Karuna, author.
Title: The Battle / Karuna Riazi.
Description: New York : Salaam Reads / Simon & Schuster Books for Young Readers, 2019. | Sequel to: The gauntlet. | Summary: A virtual reality game freezes time in New York City and thrusts twelve-year-old Ahmad Mirza and his classmate, Winnie, into the game world of Paheli, where they must overcome the Mastermind and the Architect.
Identifiers: LCCN 2019001351 (print) | LCCN 2019002746 (eBook)
| ISBN 9781534428720 (hardback) | ISBN 9781534428737 (pbk) |
ISBN 9781534428744 (eBook)
Subjects: | CYAC: Adventure and adventurers—Fiction. | Virtual reality—Fiction. | Games—Fiction. | Magic—Fiction. | Bangladeshi Americans—Fiction. | Muslims—United States—Fiction. | Upper East Side (New York, N.Y.)—Fiction. | New York (N.Y.)—Fiction. | BISAC: JUVENILE FICTION / Action & Adventure / General. | JUVENILE FICTION / Fantasy & Magic. | JUVENILE FICTION / People & Places / Middle East. Classification: LCC PZ7.1.R498 (eBook) | LCC PZ7.1.R498 Bat 2019 (print) | DDC [Fic]—dc23
LC record available at https://lccn.loc.gov/2019001351

To every reader who unknowingly held my hand through the journey of forging a second book with the eager question, "When is the next one coming out?" This one's for you, because of you. It is your personal win, and I wish you many more of them.

The game has a mind of its own.
But so do you.

THE BATTLE

CHAPTER ONE

I SWEAR I DIDN'T DO it. That's what you want to hear from me, right?"

At twelve years old, Ahmad Mirza probably shouldn't have been used to roundtable interrogations. Or know from experience what your captors wanted to hear before they would let you out from under the lights aimed at your face. "I mean, sneaking around and stealing isn't part of my daily routine."

It was the usual setup. The same old faces were clustered in the conference room, all wearing various expressions of dismay. Mrs. Evans, his homeroom teacher, clung to her coffee mug like it was a lifesaver and she was a woman overboard. Mr. Willis, the art teacher who always wore a jolly expression and cheerily arranged dreadlocks, seemed abnormally grim.

The door creaked open ominously, and Ms. Mallory, the nosy office secretary, peered in. "Do you still need the vice principal, Mr. Willis?" she asked.

Her voice sounded a little too eager, in Ahmad's opinion. Resentment bubbled up and he tried to push it down. Today wasn't an ordinary day. Today, he might have already pushed the limits of any patience PS 54 had for Ahmad Mirza and his escapades. But he ended up blurting it out anyway.

"Go ahead, Ms. Mallory. You can bring the torture devices too, but I won't talk."

Mr. Willis sighed heavily. "No, we don't need him, Ms. Mallory. Just . . . close the door."

Ms. Mallory shot Ahmad a giddy smile as she did just that. She was probably off to make sure she still had Ahmad's parents on speed dial, and she probably did.

He didn't want to think about that, though. That started the squirming up again, and the shaking in his legs that would reach his voice and really prove his false bravado to be just that: an act. Even if this was

Ahmad's normal—lunch detention and angry teachers—he didn't want to look his mother in the eyes and tell her he messed up again.

"This sucks," Ahmad mumbled to himself.

Especially because today—for once—it wasn't his fault. There had been no fight over the contents of his lunch box, no classmate leaning in and jeering at the green chili–spiked mashed potatoes that made your nose sting with the scent of fresh mustard-seed oil, or the little dried fish even he hated with eyes and silvery scales still intact.

He'd managed to be mostly respectful during class discussions, and kept his hands and feet to himself during gym. He'd even raised his hand a few times in the name of being helpful and passing out pencils, though he wasn't called on.

But in spite of all that, here he was. It didn't feel fair.

Particularly today. Because whether Mr. Willis and Mrs. Evans believed it or not . . .

"It's really not my fault," he tried again. "I don't even know how it got here."

It was the package currently resting in front of Mrs.

Evans on the table. It was an innocent yellow mailer, sealed over with Scotch tape. Nothing about it said anything like DANGER or DEVASTATING REPORT CARD INSIDE. It looked like, if you turned it over, it would be something boring like his baba's tax papers or maybe a trinket Ma ordered from overseas.

It was nothing special. At least on the outside.

Now Mrs. Evans heaved a heavy sigh. She reached for the package, tilting it downward so that its contents could slide into her palm.

"Be careful!" Ahmad gasped in spite of himself, leaning forward in his seat. Mrs. Evans shot him a dirty look but worked it out more carefully.

Though Ahmad had held it himself just half an hour ago, the sight of it made his heart lurch. It was a shiny game case, the type that held a Nintendo Switch cartridge. The cover, though, wasn't the usual 3-D characters with smiling faces and multicolored backgrounds. It was pitch black, with embossed neon images—thin lined and finely detailed, like hand sketches—on its front. What looked like flying cars and, amazingly, rickshaws were etched over a skyline that looked almost like New York City.

At least, if New York City had buildings even more futuristic than the skyscrapers Ahmad passed on his way to school.

Even though he couldn't see the title clearly from where Mrs. Evans held it to the light, he still mouthed it, quietly, to himself.

"*The Battle.*"

Mrs. Evans let out a hiss, startling both him and Mr. Willis, who leaned forward with a frown.

"Everything all right, Mrs. Evans?" he asked.

She frowned down at the game. "Yes. I think it was just static electricity."

"It's not just that," Ahmad blurted out, even though inside his brain was chanting, *Shut up, shut up, SHUT UP, Ahmad.* "It probably doesn't like you."

"Ahmad, really." His teacher leaned forward and waved the game in his face. "Okay. For the last time, tell me what this is."

"A video game," Ahmad responded. It was getting harder to control his snarky tongue and fidgety feet. He was usually better at this. He was. But the fact that they had been here a half hour and he still couldn't tell his side of the story was rattling him. "Honestly,

I've told you this like twenty times now. I don't know where it came from."

Except, of course, he did. Sort of.

"That's not what you told us before, Mirza."

"I did tell you that! I don't know why I have it. Really, I don't."

"You also told me," Mr. Willis broke in, "that the game belonged to you."

Ahmad stuck his chin out. "That's because it does."

"The question is, Mirza," Mrs. Evans snapped, "how you knew for sure this was your video game, and—more importantly—how a video game that apparently belongs to you was delivered to the school office this morning to begin with!"

Ahmad had no idea himself, though he'd glanced over the package probably a thousand times since it was first shoved into his hands a few hours ago. His sister's name and school were neatly printed on the return address—Farah Mirza, care of Princeton University.

His big sister was known for being . . . well, hard to predict. But this was mysterious, even for her. Sending a package straight to his school, without any warning?

"Ahmad, I'm about ready to get the principal in here

himself and suspend you," Mrs. Evans interrupted. "We know what's in the package, and that it's from your sister. And you have no idea why she sent it to school?"

"My sister does what she wants," Ahmad said firmly, and not without a little pride. The next part was harder to ease out, but he managed it, his fingers fidgeting in his lap. "Well, I mean, we did talk a lot about, you know. School. And friends. And how I didn't really have any. She might've wanted to . . . I don't know."

And he really didn't know. Not having friends had never been a problem his sister faced. For him, though, it was his entire life.

"Okay, then," Mrs. Evans sighed. "Let's leave your sister alone for now. What I want to know is how much nerve you have, Mr. Mirza, to sneak out and steal a package from the school office when you were supposed to be in lunch detention."

"Okay. Okay. Listen." Ahmad closed his eyes and took a deep breath, trying to steady his voice and his thick tongue. "I'm not sure why you keep saying the word 's-steal.' How could I steal it if it was mine?"

Ahmad's voice broke on the last word, and he could feel his face flush. He tried to pretend he was good at this—the whole bad boy routine—because people seemed to expect it of him. His parents no longer hugged him about the shoulders and patted his back and told him tomorrow would be better. His aunt Zohra wouldn't call and anxiously shuffle about with offers to help with his homework. (As if she knew as much about pre-algebra and auxiliary verbs as she did about Turkish puzzle rings and weird facts about Middle Eastern architecture.)

If anything, a suspension no longer meant one of his parents would take off in order to collect him. His weird, goofy uncle Vijay would—and that meant never leaving school without being more embarrassed than he ever felt before in his life.

He was the Mirza who came home with urgent notes at the bottom of his report card in red ink. The one who spent lunch with his stomach growling because the contents of his box had already been mopped off the cafeteria floor.

But he didn't like being that Mirza.

Mr. Willis, as always, came to the rescue. He put a firm hand on Ahmad's shoulder.

"Never mind that, Mrs. Evans. Look. Ahmad. We

can address everything else with your parents. But I am terribly curious to know how the boy I left at the door of lunch detention managed to zip back down to the office, rummage through staff mail, and get back upstairs in time to get himself in a world of trouble."

"You say that like it isn't a normal thing," Ahmad muttered, but he shifted uncomfortably in his chair. Ahmad wished he could tell them. He wished he could spin out the whole yarn, with every snag and loose end, and assure them that for once it was entirely, one hundred percent true.

But they couldn't believe him.

How could they, when he couldn't believe himself?

"See, the thing is . . ."

He worked his lip between his teeth. How could he put it, without being accused of another tall tale dedicated to excusing whatever trouble his fidgety body and overactive brain had steered him into?

"Look. I really didn't go into the office. Mr. Willis even said it! I didn't have time to."

"Okay," Mrs. Evans said cautiously. Mr. Willis leaned closer.

"It was more of a . . . well, someone made sure I

got the delivery, while I was still in the hallway."

"You mean, another student?" Mr. Willis's voice was full of doubt, and Ahmad's heart sank. He could see it in his teacher's eyes: *Who in this school cares that much about you?*

"I mean . . . well, um . . ."

It was no use. His mind had skittered off track. He banged his fist on the table, fighting back tears. This always happened. He started out sharp and snarky— and then, when he actually needed to be able to say something, it all just fizzled out. Poof!

After another heavy minute Mr. Willis sighed and leaned back.

"Well, that's that. Mrs. Evans, I hope you don't mind excusing Ahmad for the rest of the day. He's going to spend some quality time in here thinking about how he can explain this to us."

"But . . . the project!" Ahmad burst out, unable to help himself. His heart sank. Today was the day that art class projects were announced, and those were legendary.

"Don't worry, you're not going to miss out on all of it," Mr. Willis said, frowning. "But there is a problem.

We're doing it in partnered pairs this time, so unless someone nominates you during class, you'll have extra work to make up."

Ahmad sank down in his seat. This day had just gone from bad to worse.

"This isn't fair," he mumbled. "It really isn't fair."

"I wish I could make an exception and let you come back to class," Mr. Willis continued, "but the fact that you won't tell us the whole story—"

Behind them, the door to the conference room shot open. Mr. Willis, his mouth still open, whirled around. Mrs. Evans gasped and nearly dropped her coffee mug.

"Winnie? What are you doing out of class?"

Ahmad stared as Winnie Williamson—straight-A student and pride of the seventh-grade class—stepped through the doorway. Her brown cheeks were slick with sweat and her dark halo of curls were mussed about her face.

She looked nervous, entirely different from the girl who had rushed toward him earlier as Mr. Willis paused to speak to another teacher. That moment, when she pressed the package between his fingers and whispered, "This is yours," her entire face had been glowing.

"Well, you see . . ." Winnie hesitated for a moment, her hands balled in fists at her sides. And then, almost the way Ahmad would, she just blurted it out.

"Mr. Willis, I'm Ahmad's partner in crime. And I want to be his partner for the project, too!"

CHAPTER TWO

Y OU KNOW, YOU DON'T have to follow me all the
way home—unless you aren't done with getting
me in trouble today."

Winnie Williamson nearly knocked over the city
trash can she was casually standing behind. Ahmad
waited, trying his best not to squirm in sympathy as
she shook off a McDonald's wrapper clinging to her
sleeve and smoothed down her curls.

"I'm not following you! We just happen to be walking in the same direction."

But Winnie wouldn't quite look him in the eye.
Ahmad felt exasperation writhing like a trampled
snake in his gut. It helped loosen his tongue.

"You live four blocks down from school, Winnie,

in Lenox Hill. And this is Central Park. You actually walked past your building to keep on following me!"

"I needed fresh air," Winnie insisted, her fingers still busily fluttering to her hair, and then down to check her pockets. "And . . . well, I guess I wanted to make sure you were okay. After everything that happened earlier."

Ahmad was not okay. He was entirely done with today. Sure, it hadn't been as bad as it could be. He escaped with only a few hours of solitude and no parental intervention. But at what cost? He wasn't sure.

And now, Winnie Williamson was following him home, occasionally leaping behind utility poles and stationary taxis like a spy for the CIA. And that wasn't even the strangest part of the day. Winnie Williamson had, apparently, snuck a package out of the school office for him. Winnie Williamson, who had never even acted like she knew he was alive, had burst into a conference room and told two of their teachers that she was his partner in crime. And that whatever punishment he got, they better be ready to give her as well. He still couldn't believe it.

"Why do you care?" Ahmad mumbled gruffly. "You didn't get in trouble."

Of course she hadn't. Mr. Willis hadn't even *believed* she was part of the situation. He only frowned and shook his head.

"Winnie, I know you're always ready to stand up for a classmate in need, and I appreciate that. But Ahmad has committed a serious action with serious consequences. I want you to head back to class."

Winnie said nothing. She just looked at Ahmad, and all he could do was stare back at her. He wasn't sure what she was up to. Winnie Williamson and Ahmad Mirza lived in entirely different worlds. There were many days where he wished they didn't, where he wanted them to at least share the same space for an hour so maybe they could talk.

Maybe they could become friends.

Even with that silent hope, he never pictured her rushing up to him in an otherwise deserted hallway, pressing a yellow envelope in his hands, and whispering, "This is yours."

But she had.

"Even if I didn't get in trouble," Winnie said,

snatching him back to the street corner they stood on, "I wanted to make sure you didn't get into it either. I was in the office and just saw your name on it. It seemed like it was important, and I really didn't think it was going to be such a big deal."

"Of course you didn't." Ahmad couldn't keep some of that familiar sass off his tongue. Winnie didn't have to do that long, eyes-down shuffle through the hall every afternoon with a teacher's hand pressed on her shoulder. Winnie's conversations with teachers were all smiles, and "Yes, Mrs. Evans" and "Of course, Mr. Willis." How would she ever begin to imagine how different their experiences were?

Winnie scuffed her sneakers against the ground. In a soft mumble Ahmad wasn't sure he was meant to hear, she added, "It just seemed like the right thing to do at the time."

Before he could respond, though, Winnie seemed to realize where they were. "Hey. This isn't your way home either."

Ahmad rolled his eyes, stopping in front of an empty park bench. Around this time of day, people were still trickling out of work and school. There was hardly anyone around, except a few old ladies gossiping and one or two joggers. He slid off his backpack and sat down beside it.

"I needed some fresh air."

Winnie leaned forward, pushing an errant curl behind her ear. Ahmad instinctively pressed his back to the bench.

"What?"

"You're going to open that package, aren't you?" Her eyes sparkled with anticipation.

"Why do you care so much?" Ahmad hugged his arms around his waist, hiding the fact that, yes, his Nintendo Switch was already in his hands. The cartridge was plugged in, and the game loading. But he wasn't ready to share. He didn't know why, but he felt like he needed time to examine it on his own, before his parents (or anyone else!) got involved. He was sure school had already made that traitorous call home. Or maybe Farah had returned to dutiful daughter mode and told on herself. Being able to check it out before it was confiscated felt important.

But it wasn't only that. It was the way it *felt* when he held it. There was an electric spark when he had his hands on the case, like putting a finger on a frayed wire or touching a doorknob after shuffling over a fluffy carpet. It didn't just feel like a regular old game.

It felt like there was something alive in there.

Winnie put her hands on her hips. "I helped you get that, if you remember."

"It's not like I asked you to!" Ahmad blurted out. He could feel his ears turning red. *Keep going, Ahmad. Just dig the hole. Remind her who you are and why no one sticks around you too long.* "And besides, even if I did, why would you go ahead and do that? It's not like we're f-friends or anything."

Winnie paused. And then, there was that radiant, dimpled smile she seemed to reserve only for teachers. "Who says we aren't?"

Before he could properly respond to that, she was settling down next to him, without even asking. He had to shuffle away quickly before their elbows bumped. He plopped down on the nearest bench.

She followed and frowned down at the screen.

"This was a cartridge game, right? Why is it taking so long to load?"

"Maybe you were rough with it while you were playing Robin Hood earlier," Ahmad grumbled, but without much heat to it.

She said they were *friends*. Since when, and how? Ahmad was too embarrassed to admit that he had no experience with friends to his teachers, much less perfect Winnie Williamson. He tried to think back over the previous days and weeks but was interrupted by Winnie's whisper.

"*Paheli*."

At the same moment, there was a wash of scent in the air. Cardamom and scalded milk, with a deep musky undercurrent—like a favorite uncle's leather jacket slung carelessly over your shoulders when you were cold, bearing with it the remnants of his last cup of chai and maybe a sweet crumbling in the bottom of his pockets—wafted under Ahmad's nose.

But he was stuck on the word. The hair rose on the back of his neck and he turned slowly to face her. "What did you just say?"

Winnie blinked at him. "That is what you call it, isn't it? That city you're always doodling in the margins of your notebooks."

"How did you—"

"You're not the only one who looks around during class." Winnie beamed at him. "Your drawings for art are amazing! That's why I knew we would make a great team. Are you drawing the world from this game?"

Winnie pointed downward and Ahmad followed her gaze. She was right. There were the blue-inked buildings of the skyline from his drawings on the case, and the odd flying rickshaws. When he hovered over the icon, it read in block letters: THE BATTLE.

And then, in smaller print, *Paheli awaits*.

"Is Paheli a real place or something?" asked Winnie. "Your sketches always look so real. It's amazing."

"Honestly, I always thought it was something I dreamed up," Ahmad admitted. "I traveled to India and Bangladesh as a little kid with my parents and sister. I thought Paheli was from those memories."

Except that it had always felt so *real*. Ahmad could never understand why the actual Taj Mahal and the experience of careening through Dhaka in the back of a rickshaw seemed dull and colorless in comparison to the new city cobbled together by his brain as he slept. It was a place of glittering palaces, of marble domes and marvelous creatures that he knew couldn't be found anywhere else in the world.

"I don't think it's an actual place," Ahmad said again aloud. "So this is weird."

Winnie shrugged. "Won't know until you play it, right?"

She shifted on the bench, and Ahmad prepared himself to shuffle closer to the edge, but she paused.

"Hey, what's this?" She leaned in over his shoulder. Ahmad impatiently tapped his fingers against his rectangular Switch screen to zoom in on what she noticed.

"It's really weird, but this game seemed to come with some sort of bizarre avatar system, like one for a game you would play online," Ahmad said, peering closely at the screen. "You choose them to represent your character. Oh, do you want one of the controllers?"

"Yeah!" Winnie hummed distractedly. "Is it just me, or do these avatars seem really detailed?"

"In what way?" he asked.

She leaned in and tapped against the screen. "The

hair on this one looks just like mine. All my frizzy curls. They look so real. . . ."

Ahmad looked up at her.

Winnie's brow was furrowed. "Ahmad," she said, "do you have something to tell me?"

Oh no.

He knew that tone of voice.

It was the same tone Mrs. Evans used on him when she had her doubts about who actually started the skirmish at the lunch table or threw an eraser at her back when she was writing on the board.

"No. Like what?"

"You were just freaking out at me for following you home, but this avatar on the screen totally looks like me! It's even the same shade of brown as me. Did you talk to your sister about me or something?"

"I didn't! I swear!" Ahmad spluttered. "I just—it doesn't really look like you." But he had to admit, it certainly did.

Winnie raised her eyebrows and tapped her finger against the screen. Under her touch, the avatar twitched and shook out its—her—fluffy tight curls in a very Winnie way.

"Well, maybe it does, but I really don't know how! Honest, I don't!"

Ahmad really didn't. He wasn't the type of kid who was in school plays or exhibitions, so Farah had no opportunity to size up his schoolmates. Besides, this type of deliberate friendship arranging was more of Ma's embarrassing style.

But it was bothering him now: How could this be?

Before either of them could say more, though, the machine in Ahmad's lap caught their attention. "It's ready," Winnie whispered.

Ahmad took a deep breath and clicked start. For a moment, the screen flickered—and then returned to the same menu. He growled in frustration. "All that time and it won't even turn on?"

"Let me try," Winnie said, and took the Switch from his hands. She tapped one of the avatars—the girl that she said looked just like her—and dragged it to the center of the screen.

They waited one moment.

Two.

Ahmad shook his head.

"Forget it. Nothing's working right today."

He reached out to take the machine back from Winnie. Their hands met over the avatar.

With a sudden crackle and pop, the machine's screen went dark.

And around them, the world froze.

CHAPTER THREE

AHMAD DIDN'T NOTICE IT at first. He was too busy smacking the back of his Switch.

"No, no, no! Please don't do this to me!"

He tried to tug out the cartridge, but it was good and stuck. Maybe it had been jammed in too tight, or Farah had sent him a bootleg of some sort. His thoughts jittered and jostled against themselves in his head.

"Ahmad?"

It didn't help that Winnie's voice had suddenly risen several octaves. Ahmad shook his head, pressing the power button.

"Why . . ."

"Ahmad!" Winnie shook his arm.

"What?" Ahmad snapped, raising his head. "Gimme a minute. And stop shouting in my ear."

His voice trailed off as his eyes finally took in the world around him. The sun was still shining, and Winnie's hand on his arm still sent little shocks of disbelief into his brain. So it took him a full minute to realize what was wrong.

For the first time in Ahmad's life, Central Park was entirely still.

Nothing moved: not the pigeons dotting the pavement or the jogger in the distance, or the tree branches above their heads. Nearby, a mom leaning over a stroller did not lift her head, though her neck was craned at an awkward angle. The ice cream vendor's mouth was frozen as he shouted a greeting to the unmoving businessman strolling by with a newspaper under his arm. A dog floated in midair with his paws off the ground, lunging for a Frisbee. As Ahmad and Winnie watched in horror, he did not show any signs of plummeting back to the ground.

"What's going on?" Ahmad breathed.

"It's like someone hit a pause button," Winnie

whispered back. But her hush was as loud as a shout. There was nothing to compete with: no honking taxis or loud radios. "But why? How could this happen?"

Ahmad opened his mouth to respond. "Ouch, ouch, ouch! That hurts!"

His Switch clattered out of his fingers and onto the pavement. Winnie seized his hand, turning it back and forth. "What happened?"

Ahmad yanked it away, sticking his fingers in his mouth.

"Ith burnth me," he mumbled. A very small part of his brain was pointing out that Winnie Williamson was concerned about him, but the rest of him was too freaked out to care. In his twelve years on earth, three things remained a constant: his family, his game consoles, and his beautiful city. And suddenly, two out of three were changing the rules without warning.

What was going on?

"Oh my God, Ahmad!" Winnie exclaimed, and pointed at the ground. Ahmad's gaze followed her finger. The Switch, which had cracked against the concrete, was bleeding what appeared to be black blood.

The dark mass spread out in a puddle, and Winnie tugged Ahmad up with her so that they both stood on the bench, hugging each other.

"Is it supposed to do that?" Winnie asked.

"I—I don't think so."

One time when their parents were out at Baba's office Christmas party, Farah and Ahmad had done a classic monster mash marathon. They'd watched *Frankenstein*, *Dracula*, *Creature from the Black Lagoon*, and *The Blob*. That last movie had been funny to Ahmad at the time. Who got scared of something that looked as easily smashable as Silly Putty?

He understood it now—especially when the black . . . whatever it was . . . reached the edge of the sidewalk, and started creeping *up*, skyward, forming a wall of darkness in the midst of all the stillness. A low whine buzzed through the air, which itself was picking up into a fierce wind, blowing their hair over their eyes.

"I don't like this," Winnie whispered beside him. "Ahmad, pinch me."

She extended her arm in front of him, without even turning to look and see how he reacted.

"What? Why?"

"That's what you do when you can't wake up from a dream, right? This has to be a dream. No, it's more than a dream. It's a punishment, because I—" She clamped her lips tight and squeezed her eyes shut. "Just pinch me, Ahmad. Please."

Ahmad swallowed hard. The little experience he had in friendship, based off enviously observing his sister and her best friends, hadn't prepared him for a moment like this. Still, the black mass continued to spread, bending and warping around them to form a dark chamber. If this actually was a dream and waking Winnie up would rescue them both from it, he had to listen to her.

Tentatively he closed the tips of his fingers around her arm. "Does that work?"

Winnie's eyelids fluttered, and when they opened, she looked like her usual determined self. "Not in the way I wanted, but it does prove it isn't a dream."

"Why?"

"The Ahmad I might have expected in a dream would pinch harder."

Before Ahmad could ask what *that* even meant,

there was a resounding crackle. The black "walls" around them shimmered and popped with static, like a television screen.

An oversized head bobbed to life from the scattered pixels.

For a moment, Ahmad thought he was seeing something from *The Wizard of Oz*: that horrible face surrounded by green flames. But it wasn't a mysterious, wizened wizard. It was a girl. She looked around their age, with a long pale white face, short blond hair, and a leopard print hat jammed over her ears. A lollipop rolled around her lips as she smirked at them.

"Hello," she purred. "That took a little while to boot up. I was supposed to do a trial run earlier, but I don't believe in trial runs. It's better to just launch in and figure it out as you go, right?"

Ahmad and Winnie blinked at her.

"What—" Ahmad started. "What are you?"

The girl deliberately lifted a hand and turned it in front of her eyes.

"Well, I'm not sure how native they are to your area of the world, but where I come from, I'm called a human. Also known as Homo sapiens."

"You're not cute," Winnie broke in harshly. Her cheeks were flushed, and her chest heaved. "Is this some sort of prank? Did you really waste a ton of money on some special effects and a projector or whatever this is to freak out two kids on their way home from school?"

She looked angrier than Ahmad had ever seen her. It was both awe-inspiring and a little scary.

The girl on the screen did not look as impressed. "And here I thought I wouldn't need a monologue to get you guys started. What a waste of my time. If some people would just do their job . . . Okay, listen up."

She clapped her hands. Out of nowhere, there was the ear-popping wail of sirens and a canned applause track. Ahmad covered his ears and Winnie jumped, nearly jostling him off the bench.

"What was that for?"

"Congratulations!" the girl said cheerily. "You two are the latest in a long and privileged line to play one of the oldest and most exciting games the world has ever known, in its newest and finest rendition. Thanks of course, to yours truly, the MasterMind!"

On the large, floating screen formed the blue, sparking words from Ahmad's game cover:

THE BATTLE.

The words faded, giving way to a brief jumble of images: marble palaces, lush green courtyards, and an aerial view of a skyline that seemed more suited to India than New York City. Ahmad's heart pounded.

"Why does this all look so familiar?" he mumbled. He felt like he knew what the MasterMind was going to say next as she gloated about "state-of-the-art" levels and "immersive technology."

"The great city of Paheli," he mouthed.

And he was right.

". . . meaning that the great city of Paheli is bigger and better than ever," the hologram girl gushed. "All new and upgraded for the twenty-first century."

Before Ahmad could say anything, Winnie interrupted, her eyes wide. "Paheli? You mean, Ahmad's Paheli? Do you really expect us to believe this?"

Before Ahmad could stop her, she hopped nimbly off the park bench. They both flinched as a sharp crack came from beneath her sneakers. The MasterMind gave a frustrated howl. "Look what you've done now!"

Winnie gingerly lifted her heel. Beneath it, the

black mass had shattered like the glass on a dropped phone screen. She looked at Ahmad with wide eyes. "This is real. It's not special effects."

"It's *my* screen, and now I'm going to have to waste time on repairs," the girl seethed. "Oh, you're going to be so sorry once the game's started."

Ahmad's heart was lodged in his throat. All of this felt so familiar in the worst way: games, and players, and *Paheli*. "This is real, Winnie," he mumbled. "All of this is real. I don't know how I know, but it is."

"Ahmad, are you serious?" Winnie flung out her arm toward the screen surrounding them on all sides. "This has to be a prank. It *has to be*. This weirdo heard us talking about Paheli just now and set up this whole reality TV show nonsense. This can't be real."

"Look at his face," the MasterMind jeered. "It's starting to sink in for him, at least. But if you don't want to believe me without some further evidence . . ."

She waved a hand, and the screen directly in front of them shimmered out of existence. Disappeared into thin air. They were once again staring out across their frozen city.

"What—" Winnie started, but a rustling in the tree beside them had Ahmad seizing her arm. Something felt very, very wrong.

"Ask *him* if he's made of smoke and mirrors," the MasterMind's voice floated over them.

And then Winnie let out a shriek. "What is that?"

Crawling deliberately down the trunk, every one of its beady eyes trained on them, was the biggest spider Ahmad had ever seen in his life—at least, while he was awake. He was sure he'd seen it in a nightmare one time, only different. With a metallic sheen to its fangs and an odd hum of a voice.

Its back bristled with tan hairs, and with every step something seemed to pop and slide off them. Whatever it was crackled under the monster's feet as it moved forward.

"Sand," Ahmad said softly, another of his strange dream-details popping into place. "Everything in Paheli is made of sand. This is a sand spider!"

Winnie jerked him backward, her eyes glancing about wildly for some form of escape. "Okay!" she yelled. "Okay, we get it. This is real. Now make it stop!"

"Already?" The girl's disembodied voice sounded disappointed. "And you haven't even given him a chance to have a taste."

But she snapped her fingers, and the spider dissipated into a pile of dust.

Winnie slowly walked forward until the tip of her sneaker was in the dust. She kicked it tentatively, watching the dust rise, and then looked up at the screen.

"Okay. So this *is* real. But what if we decide not to play this game of yours? Will you just keep generating scary spiders to rush at us?"

"That does sound like an idea," the MasterMind said, giving a horrible grin that made Ahmad shudder. "But I'd say the stakes are higher. I won't give away too much, because what's the fun in that? I will tell you, though, that the game tends to hold on to the players who can't make it past the finish line."

That sounded bad enough.

And then a horrible thought occurred to Ahmad.

"This park . . . is the only place frozen right now, right? Our parents must be missing us."

That was an understatement. Honestly, his parents probably called the police by this point. Ahmad's heart squeezed. It was just another way to disappoint them. But the MasterMind only smiled.

"Are you kidding me?" The MasterMind rolled her eyes. "Wake up and get with the program. *Of course they are frozen.* You see, I'm the type of girl who goes for big plans. If I have to freeze any corner of this grubby, crumbling city you call home, why not take it all? And then maybe the entire world?"

She waved her hand, and her face faded to an aerial view of the city. Ahmad and Winnie gasped in horror. It was *all* frozen. New York City, the city that never slept, was as still as a cemetery. Tourists' feet hovered over crosswalks and little kids skipped in midair, never landing.

"Go big, or go home," the MasterMind said smugly as they stared at her handiwork.

Winnie dug her fingers into Ahmad's arm. "My parents," she whispered.

Ahmad stared at the screen, at the cheery couple in the middle of their kitchen. Winnie's father was still reaching toward an open cabinet for a set of dishes.

Winnie's mother was frozen in laughter, her head thrown back.

The screen flashed, cutting to his house.

"No one's home," Ahmad whispered as the camera panned over the pristine hallway and through the kitchen. But then, it reached the living room.

Ma leaned on the vacuum cleaner, her brow puckered with worry. Perhaps that had been the moment she realized he wasn't home yet, or maybe the bag inside the machine had overflowed again. Maybe she was about to put it away entirely and call the school. But she stood there, still as stone.

Baba sat on the couch, cell phone to his ear and a newspaper held between one stiff hand. The camera moved up to take in his half-open mouth, his eyes glancing downward to read something off the page.

Anger welled up in Ahmad. "Why did you have to do this to them?" he yelled. "If you want us to play the game, fine. But why involve our parents?"

"That would be telling, wouldn't it," the MasterMind's ghostly voice came. "But now, the ball is in your court. I think you've seen enough to realize what the right decision is."

The screen parted in its middle, forming a doorway. Through the shimmering vortex at its center, Ahmad could just make out the park and its frozen trees and . . . His eyes narrowed. No, there was something different about that park on the other side.

The MasterMind's parting words floated over them.

"Paheli awaits. Enjoy every last drop of it. . . ."

CHAPTER FOUR

S O WHAT DO WE do now?" Winnie said, rubbing
her hands up and down her arms.

It wasn't remotely cold, but Ahmad understood why she was doing it. After the MasterMind's
hologram had disappeared, the black mass had seeped
down into the ground. They were no longer boxed in,
but around them, Central Park was still caught in that
horrible, silent stillness. He had the shivers too.

It didn't help that the doorway was still looming in
front of them.

"What else can we do?" Ahmad asked back. "We
play the game."

It was weird, but unlike Winnie, he wasn't in shock.
Instead, all that he could feel was a cold, hard knot of

anger in the pit of his stomach. His parents' frozen faces hung in front of his mind's eye.

They didn't ask for this.

And he couldn't let them down. Not again.

No, there was no other choice. They had to do this.

Winnie didn't seem to think the same way though. She stared at him with wide eyes.

"Ahmad, are you kidding me? We're *kids*. Shouldn't we call the police? Or maybe someone at school."

"Like anyone at school would believe me!" Ahmad burst out. His hands clenched into fists at his side. "Like any adult—if they aren't Popsicles right now—would believe this could even happen. Winnie, you saw the spider. You saw our parents." He waved his arms around, gesturing to the still life of Central Park. "We don't have anyone to rely on in this but us."

He bit back the words that were coming next: "*I know that better than anyone else.*"

"Ahmad," Winnie said softly. There was a look in her eyes that he didn't like: the same look teachers gave him the day before a parent-teacher conference or when, even with extra time to finish a test, he struggled for the right words to write down.

It was pity.

"No matter how we do it, we need to play," Ahmad said firmly, before she could say anything else. "We need to do this for our parents, and we need to do this for ourselves. I don't think we can count on anyone else."

"We can count on each other," Winnie replied. She reached out and gently pressed her hand against his arm. "We're going to do this together. As long as you can promise me that, I'm in."

Ahmad looked her in the eye for a long moment. And then he nodded. "Together." The word felt unfamiliar in his mouth.

They awkwardly grasped each other's hands and turned to face the shimmering doorway left behind by the MasterMind's screen.

They stepped forward, bracing themselves on each other, and looked downward as the wind lashed at their hair and faces—thankfully, free of sand for the moment. There was a small platform waiting for them. Together, they leapt down.

As the wind whooshed hot and heavy into Ahmad's ears and head, he thought he heard a familiar voice call to him from the stillness they'd left behind. A voice that said, "Don't go—"

But it was too late now. Because they were falling.

Falling.

Falling.

Longer than they should have been. But then Ahmad felt his feet settle on solid ground, and looked down.

If New York City could see what was below them, it would wither with envy—because the city they gazed at was *gorgeous*.

The city from the game rose up with elaborate floating skyscrapers that reminded Ahmad of the pictures he'd seen of Dubai. The occasional faint glimmer of an anchorless oasis darted in and out between the unmoored buildings. Laughter bobbed up to them on the breeze, broken through with snatches of songs. There were tunes Ahmad could recognize from his aunt's favorite Bollywood films and his father's classic Bengali music CDs, smuggled back to the States under layers of his uncle's clothing and homemade sweets.

They leaned back into the doorway to avoid a stray flying rickshaw, skittering forward with no visible driver, and a passenger shrouded in gloom behind the thick curtain within its carriage. Ahmad, though, couldn't crane his head like Winnie to try and curiously ogle the person within.

Not when he saw it.

"No way," Ahmad said breathlessly, his eyes drinking in the sight of a gilded, glowing funicular rail. It was right in the place where he had once sketched it out on a stray piece of notebook paper during math class. It was right where it had always been in those dreams.

Just beyond it, at the very center of the digital city, was a minaret, tall and towering, glimmering at its tip with a green flame.

Glowing words bobbed just above it: WELCOME TO PAHELI.

"It is my Paheli," Ahmad mumbled to himself. "But . . . how?"

"Hey, Ahmad, you okay? The height getting to you?" Winnie placed her hand on Ahmad's shoulder. He hadn't realized until that moment that he was swaying back and forth.

"It's not—it's just—"

Of course, this would be the moment that his traitor tongue started its stumbling routine again.

"It's Paheli," Ahmad said again, looking into Winnie's worried brown eyes. "Not entirely the way I've always pictured it, with all this high-tech stuff and the flying cars. But it's here. And I don't know why."

Winnie was silent for a moment. "Isn't this amazing, though?"

Ahmad looked up in surprise. Winnie's brown face glowed, that familiar smile stretching from ear to ear.

"It's your dream world, brought to life!" She spread out her arms and spun, teetering dangerously close to the doorway.

Ahmad tossed out a hand. "Be careful! Gosh, Winnie."

"Relax. Okay, maybe 'relax' isn't the right word," she said. "Yes, things are terrible right now. But did you ever think you'd see your city—your Paheli—alive like this? It's amazing! And it's yours!"

This was the last reaction Ahmad possibly expected from Winnie Williamson. She reached out and pressed down on his shoulders, turning him back to face Paheli.

"Look at it," she said, and Ahmad tried to see it through her eyes.

Maybe she was right, a little.

Yes, the domes were shot through with pulsing electric veins and the palaces tugged at their roots and floated up in the air. But it was still familiar.

More alien and weird was the fact that Winnie Williamson was holding his shoulder and he didn't feel squirmy and awkward and wrong-footed. He felt comforted. He felt like he wasn't alone.

Was this what it felt like to have a friend? He still wasn't sure, but he was glad Winnie was with him. For now, that was enough.

"Yeah," Ahmad said softly. "Yeah, it really is awesome."

They stared together in silence for a moment. Ahmad cleared his throat. "So, uh, any ideas on what we should do now?"

"Well, we need to play whatever this game is," Winnie said thoughtfully. "And we can't do that by just standing here and staring at Paheli from a distance."

She hummed to herself for a moment, watching as a train slithered through the air beneath them like a serpentine dragon. When she looked back up, there was a glimmer in her eye that made Ahmad suddenly uneasy.

"What?" He backed up slightly. "Winnie, what are you planning?"

"It's not really a plan. It's more like following an instinct, and a rule of the universe." Winnie reached out and grabbed up his hand.

"Winnie, I don't think this is a good idea."

"What goes up, must come down!" Winnie giddily cried.

Someone else cried out with her. At the moment, Ahmad was sure it was his brain. It was too quick and too far to tell, anything but the one word shouted.

"*Wait!*"

And she jumped.

Down Ahmad went with her, shrieking.

Tumbling into the lyrical lights and foreboding shadows.

Hurtling into the canals of both stone and clockwork, the hologram swords that cut through him and slid out as easily as a magician's prop, and the silk awnings over vendors' stalls.

Together they descended into the lap of the layered city, Paheli.

CHAPTER FIVE

FREE-FALLING DIDN'T FEEL THE way Ahmad always expected it to.

At least, after the first few minutes when he wildly glanced around with Winnie—locating her right at his side, screaming right along with him—and had the mental space to take in everything else going on, it didn't.

Yes, the wind tugged back his cheeks and whined past his ears. But after a few moments, when the drag on his arms and legs didn't lead to a sudden and swift crush to the ground, he was able to work open his eyes. And he looked down.

Big mistake.

Paheli was spread out beneath them. The buildings

and distant streets seemed small and delicately crafted, like they were meant to house ants.

"Okay," Ahmad shouted to Winnie, not daring to look away from the ground. "It was your bright idea to jump through the doorway. What now?"

When there was no answer, he craned his neck to the side. Winnie had her arms spread out at her sides, like she was flying. She flashed him a huge grin.

"This is better than any ride at Six Flags!"

"Are you serious? At Six Flags, there are safety belts and attendants and red emergency buttons you can push if it gets too rough. Don't you see what's under us?"

"We're playing a game. There has to be some sort of safety mechanism involved." Winnie did a somersault in midair.

She was right. There had to be some way out of this. Every good game had its utility belts and parachutes. Surely, the MasterMind didn't want them to lose, and painfully, right out of the gate.

It was then he saw it: a single, starlike glimmer off a polished metal handle.

Ahmad leaned forward, squinting his eyes against the air batting at his face.

"Is that a car?" he mumbled.

It didn't look like the cars lining the streets of New York City. Two bright red fins jutted out on either side, in the place where handles would be on the doors. The top of it too—shiny and rounded in a way that resembled a rickshaw canopy more than the hood and top of a Mustang or Honda Civic or even a vintage Volkswagen Bug—seemed like an unusual design choice.

Was it really a car at all?

Winnie tried to straighten herself out so she could look. "I mean, I think so. That's a pretty interesting look. Hey! Maybe that's our ride!"

"Our ride?" Ahmad echoed dubiously.

"Come on, start thinking like you're in a game! If it catches your eye, that means it's probably meant for us."

Ahmad blinked at her. They were kids. They didn't have driver's licenses. Why would it be meant for them?

Then again, they were currently plummeting down through space and time toward a city that had previously resided only in his dreams. There was no other time to think or question. They had to act now.

"Winnie, I think you're right! The car! It's on that

ledge we're headed toward!" he shouted. "I think our best bet is to try and land there!"

They batted their arms and flailed their legs against the thick city air. Ahmad flung out one hand. If he could only reach. There!

He caught the ledge and heard Winnie yelp as she narrowly grasped it beside him. They dragged themselves up and stared at the car. It wasn't entirely a car so much as a hybrid with one of the rickshaws that had flown past them, an awning over the body and futuristic lightning bolts on its doors. Inside, a console covered with flickering buttons mushroomed over the dashboard and seemed to grow around the steering wheel.

Ahmad and Winnie exchanged glances.

"Do you know how to drive?" Ahmad asked.

Winnie shrugged. "How hard can it be?" Looking at Ahmad's panicked face, she sighed. "Get in the car. Let's at least look for clues."

"That girl said to enjoy every drop of Paheli. I don't think that was an accident," Ahmad said, reaching for the driver's door.

Winnie climbed in on the passenger side. "What we

need is a map," she declared. She felt along the console for a glove compartment. Ahmad reached out to join her and winced as his fingers made contact with a big black button.

Uh-oh.

"Ahmad!" Winnie looked up, eyes wide, but before she could scold him, the car whirred to life beneath them. With a flash and a hum, it careened off the ledge where it had been parked and into the open air.

"We're falling!" Ahmad shouted.

Ahmad and Winnie reached for each other. Ahmad clenched his eyes shut, ready for the free fall. But it didn't come.

"Ahmad! Ahmad!" Winnie said. "Open your eyes and move so I can steer, or else we'll really be in trouble!"

Ahmad opened his eyes and gasped.

The car was *flying*. Well, it was jerking up and down, narrowly scraping against building sides and being honked at by angry rickshaw drivers teetering back and forth on their jet-powered bicycles, but it was flying.

"Ahmad. I'm not joking. Move."

Winnie sighed, exasperated. She clambered forward, taking hold of the wheel. Ahmad quickly pressed himself against the window.

"My cousin's got a go-kart," she said. "I think it's more or less the same."

"You just rolled your eyes at me when I asked you if you knew how to drive!"

"I rolled my eyes because you didn't have your priorities straight!" Winnie seemed like a different person as she studied the console. After a moment, she tentatively pressed a red button.

A screen set into the console flickered to life. It trembled with the rocking car as it announced, "Welcome to Paheli. Outside, it is ninety-eight degrees and another beautiful evening in our favorite city of riddles. If you need a tutorial to best enjoy your new vehicle—"

Winnie jammed her finger against the screen with a scowl. It went black. "I hate back-seat drivers."

But Ahmad was barely listening. He pressed his face against the window, fighting the churning of his stomach as he stared down at Paheli. It was all there: the beautiful, billowing canopies spread over stalls and tables, which, when he looked hard enough, were covered with marvelous wares and magical bags of spices.

It was the souk, the marketplace where anything could be bought.

Enjoy every drop of it, the Mastermind whispered in Ahmad's mind, and he sat upright.

"Winnie. I think I know where we're supposed to start."

"Good, because we've got company." Winnie's voice was strained, and Ahmad hastily scooted over in her direction, craning his head over her shoulder to stare out her window and see what she had. His heart sank.

"Is that . . ."

"Yep. Your dream city's law enforcement," Winnie said.

A sleek, silvery vehicle darted between buildings, like a shark determined not to be seen by the fish it was stalking. Inside its long body, Ahmad could make out the shadowy faces of two men. The sight of them did not make him reassured.

"They don't look very friendly," Winnie muttered.

"Do you think this game is programmed to welcome players? Or is it going to turn on us like antibodies in the immune system?"

"I don't think we want to find that out yet," Ahmad said. "Winnie, hover at street level."

"You don't have to tell me twice." Winnie tugged.

Ahmad's heart thumped as the memories from his sketches fell into place alongside the winding avenue. He was right.

"Take a left, and then hang a right up here. . . ."

And if you go forward and through that archway, past the stall with the hot samosas and underneath the table of the merchant with the flying carpets . . .

"There!" Ahmad caught sight of the man, tall and proud with his arms crossed, watching as a family clambered aboard a flying carpet that was woven out of elegant wiring and reinforced with steel.

Winnie's eyes widened.

Together they said, "No matter what else changes, there's always a tea shop here."

Ahmad glanced at Winnie out of the corner of his eye. "You remembered?"

Winnie gave him a surprisingly shy smile. "It's the

one landmark you always start with on your sketches in class. It's hard not to notice."

They coasted to a stop, nestled in a blanket of space cast between two rickety skyscrapers. In between them, with a neon sign worthy of a Queens street corner on a rainy night, was the tea shop.

MADAME NASIRAH'S TEA AND SNACKS.

Underneath, there was a scrolling marquee banner, which read, *Back and better than ever! Ask about our spinach pies!*

For a moment, Ahmad and Winnie just stared at the shop.

"I can't believe this," Ahmad whispered. "It *is* real."

"So, what do we do now?" Winnie asked.

"What else can we do? We have to see if the MasterMind really wanted us to end up here."

Ahmad squared his jaw and grasped the doorknob, but it swung inward before he could open it. There stood a woman. She was hidden under gauzy shawls dangling from her arms. Her face was veiled with an oversized and knotted dopatta. It didn't matter.

Because somehow, Ahmad knew exactly who she was.

CHAPTER SIX

MADAME NASIRAH," AHMAD WHISPERED in awe. "The Gamekeeper."

The woman seemed to be taken aback for a moment, before she spoke cheerily.

"Why, yes! I suppose with these new doodads . . . No, what am I supposed to call them? Upgrades, that's the word. Anyway, I'm sure they probably have instructions to keep the players' heads on straight. I am indeed Madame Nasirah, your Gamekeeper."

Winnie eyed Ahmad curiously as the woman turned to set down the tray in her hands. "But how do you know who she is?"

"I don't know," Ahmad responded. In his head,

he had always pictured Paheli with a bustling, colorful cast of characters. But he never bothered to write down the backstories and family ties he dreamed up, more focused on trying to lay out the city itself. So they tended to change every so often.

Still, though, the memory of the woman and her name had come without difficulty, and he wasn't entirely sure why. After all, a game had never been part of what he imagined about Paheli.

"Now there," Madame Nasirah said, clapping her hands free of dust before lifting the teapot off the counter. "First things first, you'll need some tea and . . ."

Somewhere behind the layers of cloth, her eyes met Ahmad's. Her hand flew up to her mouth.

"Oh! Oh my!"

The teapot Madame Nasirah held slipped from her fingers.

Crash!

"Oh no!" Winnie gasped, rushing forward to grab the woman's hand. "Are you okay?"

It was a very Winnie reaction, and it would have made Ahmad smile. Except that the woman didn't answer. She stared at the both of them, frozen. When she did move, it was in a quick rush of limbs, lunging at him with open arms.

"It can't be," she whispered. She clasped Ahmad's face between her hands. It took him a minute to realize that tears were silently dripping down her cheeks. "This shouldn't be possible."

"What are you talking about?"

Ahmad didn't do well with crying adults in general, but this was a new level of weird. He made wide, desperate eyes at Winnie, who looked just as panicked. That was a little surprising, considering how much better Winnie was with adults usually.

"Your face is so familiar," Madame Nasirah said. She leaned back and dabbed delicately at her eyes, trying to laugh. "I'm sorry, I don't know what's come over me."

Ahmad awkwardly wrapped his arm around her and gave her a few pats. Her embrace did feel familiar. She smelled of cardamom and cinnamon: like all the best desserts and his mother's favorite tea blend. But a bit deeper and mustier. *Older.*

Winnie politely cleared her throat. "Sorry to butt

in, but . . . you've seen Ahmad before? As a player?"

Madame Nasirah blinked at her. "Is Ahmad his name?" She looked back down into Ahmad's face, squinting her eyes. "If only I could recall properly. This city keeps changing its rules on me, which is not unusual for Paheli. Its name after all means . . ."

"Riddle," Ahmad finished for her. It always had been the best type of puzzle to him. He'd try to pin down the streets that were sometimes so vivid in his mind, but they seemed to change the next time he had a pencil in his hand.

"Yes." Madame Nasirah smiled fondly as she bent down to pick up the strewn pieces of the teapot. "That's Paheli for you. But recently, after this MasterMind or whoever arrived, there's all these new words to learn and sometimes you go out to find a street you could find at a particular hour has vanished entirely—"

She broke off, shaking her head.

"But oh! The tea! I'll need to put on another pot. You'll need every last drop for strength before you proceed deeper into the game."

Ahmad's eyes widened, and he glanced toward Winnie.

Enjoy every last drop.

They were definitely in the right place.

At Madame Nasirah's urging, they gingerly sat on dusty silk cushions around a small, round table. Everything about the shop, in comparison to the high-tech glamour of the street outside, seemed unloved and secondhand.

Winnie nudged Ahmad in the ribs, and hissed, "Do we really need to drink the tea?"

"The MasterMind said . . ."

"I know what she said. But how do we know it's safe for us to drink it?"

Winnie's eyes were round. Ahmad was stunned.

"Um, haven't we switched places?" he whispered. "Usually, you're Ms. 'Let's Ask the Teacher What to Do.'"

"And you were Mr. 'The Adults Can't Help Us' not more than a half hour ago!" Winnie tapped her finger on the table furiously. "How do we know this lady is actually here to help us and she's not like some minor boss we have to fight in order to search the shop for clues?"

At Ahmad's stare, she sighed exasperatedly. "You're not the only video game fan, you know."

Ahmad looked down at the table. He didn't know what else to say. She was right about him not usually being so quick to trust. But for some reason, the familiarity of the woman was sinking into his gut and warming him.

And the smell of chai in the air reminded him of home. How could he not want to take a sip?

Winnie leaned in to say something more, but a new tray settled in front of them.

"Here we are," Madame Nasirah said cheerily. "Who's going first?"

"I'm not thirsty," Winnie started, and Ahmad broke in, "I'll have some."

He focused on Madame Nasirah's smile so he didn't have to look at Winnie's dagger eyes. The warm, fuzzy feelings he'd had about the girl while they were plummeting through the air were starting to evaporate. Winnie Williamson wasn't the boss of him, and she was the one who had pointed out that this was his city.

His Paheli wouldn't hurt him. Would it?

Madame Nasirah raised the teapot so that the tea cascaded, bubbling and frothing, as it filled the glass.

"My mom's friend from Morocco pours tea like

that, but I always thought it was for fun," Ahmad said, feeling another rush of that bittersweet sense of home.

"Of course she does," Madame Nasirah said cheerily. "The tea tastes better that way."

As Ahmad slid his glass carefully toward him, the woman turned to Winnie, who looked unsure. "I'm not much of a tea person. I think I'll pass."

"Oh, come now," Madame Nasirah said impatiently. "It's a rite of passage in my shop. And you've never had my tea. Come, child. Take some."

Winnie bit her lip, but then Ahmad exclaimed in surprise, "It's chai!" He stared into his cup at the creamy, carefully spiced tea sloshing within it. "It's my ma's chai."

"My teapot knows," said Madame Nasirah, smiling at them.

Winnie held out her glass and stared at its contents as they poured in. Ahmad leaned forward to investigate. "That's not chai. But how—"

"Results may vary per player," Madame Nasirah said primly, taking back the pot and rising to her feet in order to peer at the shop's dusty counter. "Now, where did I put those spinach pies?"

Winnie wrinkled her nose down at her cup and looked up at Ahmad.

"What?" Ahmad asked.

She raised her eyebrows, glanced down at his cup, and then back up at his face.

Ahmad rolled his eyes. "It's been a few minutes now and my stomach feels fine. Come on, Winnie."

Winnie rolled her eyes right back but reached for her cup. "If I die, I'm coming back to haunt you."

She took a tentative sip. And then stared down into the cup.

"What?" Ahmad asked anxiously. "What's wrong?"

Winnie shook her head. Suddenly, she looked very small and uncertain. When she spoke, her voice was barely above a whisper.

"It tastes like the tea my mom makes on sick days," she said, biting her lip. "Dad says he married Mom knowing he would make the coffee every morning because she could burn a pot of water. She really does, every time. And then Grandma comes in quietly and does something so that it actually tastes like tea again, and just smiles and nods while Mom takes all the credit."

"Um . . . wow." Ahmad inwardly pinched himself for that lackluster response. How come he couldn't say something normal, something supportive?

It didn't seem like Winnie noticed, though.

"This morning, I was so irritated with all of them. But after seeing them frozen on the screen—after tasting the tea . . . I don't know why I was."

Madame Nasirah squeezed Winnie's shoulder. Ahmad hadn't even noticed her come back in the room. "If you want," she suggested gently, "I could pour you a fresh cup. See what else the pot could give you."

But Winnie shook her head. "This is good enough." She took another sip, blinking her eyes fiercely.

Ahmad turned to Madame Nasirah. "So you are the Gamekeeper. Does this mean you pulled us into this game?"

Madame Nasirah shook her head. "I'm merely a gatekeeper—or what is the word that dreadful girl is always using? A tutorial. I'm here to let you know the rules, and what you need to do if you hope to win. Some spinach pies, dears."

Ahmad jerked back as a plate of delightfully steaming pastries was plunked in front of him.

"Now," Madame Nasirah said, watching approvingly as Winnie stuffed a spinach pie in her mouth and hummed happily. "This game is one that only ever seeks young players. And I will tell you right now that now that it has you, it will not want to let you go. So listen carefully."

A shiver ran down Ahmad's spine.

"Paheli is a place of riddles," Madame Nasirah said softly. "This game is not a simple one of throwing dice and moving forward spaces. It is one that will require you to remember what you've seen, keep track of what is in your pockets, and know who your allies are. Even the rules I tell you now may shift."

"Wait, then," Winnie interjected around a mouthful of crumbly date cookie. "That doesn't seem fair. How are we supposed to play if the rules change on us?"

"The Architect doesn't aim to play fair. The one time he did, he lost and the whole of Paheli nearly fell apart. Now, he's learned from it. He and his new friend, that awful MasterMind, are going to be throwing everything they have at you."

"The Architect?" Ahmad's heart pounded. That was not a name he had ever made up or casually written down as an inhabitant of Paheli. It should have been unfair, and yet, somehow, when she said it, something tickled at the back of his brain: a marble palace and a cold hand on his shoulder.

Madame Nasirah snorted. "The little spoiled prince of Paheli and the originator of the game. The entire city used to quake under his terrible tantrums. He would conjure up a sandstorm if someone so much as stepped on his foot."

"He sounds lovely," Winnie said dryly, pushing a date cookie between Ahmad's fingers. He bit into it, relishing the contrast of the sandy dough against the sticky filling.

"If he's friends with the MasterMind, though, I'm not surprised. She seems like a piece of work."

"Ah, that one, I know less about." Madame Nasirah shoved a plate of kanafe that she seemed to have conjured out of nowhere toward Ahmad. He resignedly took a slice. The language of aunties was unspoken and brooked no complaint or refusal to obey. Besides, the sweet pastry was piping hot and delicious, tendrils of cheese sliding apart temptingly between his fingers.

"The game announces players' arrivals, so she

wouldn't have entered that way or I would have known myself. I'm not entirely sure how the game came back to life to begin with. The last player who won—" Madame Nasirah shook her head with a fond chuckle. "She did a good job of tearing it apart to the roots. In any case, all you need to know about both of them is that they are trouble."

Winnie leaned forward. "So, even if the rules change, there has to be something about the game that helps us figure out what we need to do, right?"

"There are three rounds," Madame Nasirah said. "Each centers on a particular puzzle that you must solve within a given amount of time. The city will be your playing board. It shifts to accommodate whatever challenge is set before you."

"Oh, great," Ahmad sighed. "And here I was hoping it'd be something like a relay race."

"I'm afraid it's not that simple," Madame Nasirah said, leaning in closer. "In any case, if you can succeed, you will earn a puzzle piece that you need to continue on. You'll know it when you see it."

A hand rose from beneath her shawls and Ahmad and Winnie gasped in amazement at the shining object held within her palm: a puzzle piece, but one carved from heavy metal and inlaid with precious stones.

"You need to be stingy with your time and careful with your trust. The people of Paheli hold loyalty to no one but the Architect, and that is merely because his whim rules their city."

Winnie looked pale. "It's so intense," she said softly. "What happens if we lose a challenge?"

"It is," Madame Nasirah replied, resting one hand on her head. "I won't lie to you and tell you that it isn't. If you lose, you're stuck here with the rest of us. But you cannot let thoughts like that cloud your judgment. You must look ahead and see the finish line without that anxiety and doubt hanging off your shoulders. You have two enemies to face as it is, Winnie. Do not let yourself become another."

Winnie swallowed hard.

Ahmad, though, leaned forward. "Where do we start?"

CHAPTER SEVEN

T HIS PLACE REALLY GIVES me the creeps," Winnie muttered under her breath as the kids edged through a crowded alleyway. Madame Nasirah had suggested a stroll through the souk so they could get their bearings before the challenges began. But Ahmad felt he couldn't quite find his footing.

"I know what you mean," Ahmad agreed.

Paheli felt like it was squirming out of its skin, right beneath their feet. Maybe it was something to do with the music track that blasted in the background, on loop like any typical video game. There was something dark and wildly violent about the distant drums and shrill flute.

It was unfair, actually, because the rest of Paheli

wasn't dark or scary or disturbing at all. The best way Ahmad could think of it was that they were underwater—at least, if the ocean floor was designed by whoever at Disney dreamed up *Tron*: all sparkle and metal surfaces, cut through with neon avenues and hologram storefronts.

Winnie darted backward, gasping, as the sweets shop they passed blinked out of existence.

"Did I do that? What just happened?"

"I don't know—" Ahmad started, and then gaped along with her as the store flickered back into existence. But something had changed. There was now a silver awning, and instead of the cheery, round-faced woman arranging frosted cakes alongside trays of syrupy orange jalebi in the window, a stern young man adjusted odd suits on shiny steel mannequins.

"How did it do that?" Ahmad whispered.

Winnie was leaning close to the window.

"What are those suits made of? I've never seen a fabric that can do that."

The suit—a simple kurta shirt over billowing pants—seemed a vibrant green at first glance. Once the kids focused, though, they could see an underlying purple paisley print, pulsing in and out of existence like a heartbeat.

"Let's see if we can make it do that again," Ahmad said eagerly, leaning forward.

The kids giggled as the shops glimmered back and forth, in and out of existence. One moment, it was the elegant clothing shop, and the next, they caught a glimpse of the woman popping a frosting-covered finger in her mouth before guiltily waving at them.

A tap on the glass startled both of them, along with a muffled "Ahem." The young man scowled at them and pointed at a sign above his head. Words glowed on it, formed by a hundred small light bulbs like the type you might see at an old-fashioned Broadway show.

"What does that say?" Winnie said, blinking rapidly. "All I see is paisley."

"Please mind our automated store," Ahmad read aloud. "If you do not wish to come inside, step back and give us time to prepare for our customers."

When Ahmad looked back at the salesman, he made a shooing motion with his hand.

"Oh, uh, sorry," Winnie mumbled, tugging Ahmad back. "Ahmad!"

Ahmad couldn't resist one last hand wave in the direction of the shop. The disapproving young man opened his mouth to protest, but in a moment, he was replaced with the charming pastel and jewel-laden cake stands of the sweets shop.

The woman looked up from her frosting with a smile, right as a group of customers wandered in.

"Ahmad," Winnie said again, trying to look disapproving. "That wasn't cool."

Ahmad shrugged. "I stopped. That's what he wanted, right?"

Winnie narrowed her eyes, though her lips were still twitching at the corners.

"You know that's not what he wanted. He was a bit snooty, but so what?"

So what was right, and Ahmad knew it. But he couldn't help himself, just like he couldn't help himself at school when a teacher said something that brought to mind a snarky comeback or a student wrinkled their nose up at his lunch.

"I said I stopped, okay?" Ahmad insisted. "I won't do it again. Sorry."

Winnie looked at him hard for a long moment,

and then relaxed into one of her easy smiles.

"Whatever. It's fine. Let's keep going."

They turned their backs on the shop.

"Automated store, huh?" Winnie said. "That is pretty cool."

"Thinking about it sounds really stressful," Ahmad responded. The man didn't look like he was ready for it to switch. Ahmad felt a guilty twinge in the pit of his stomach. "And what if someone can't decide which shop they want right away, or they step into one without realizing they stepped into the wrong shop?"

There was a sudden pop behind them.

The kids whirled around as the newly settled clothing shop gave way once again to the bakery. The lady was carefully dusting sugar over a plate of rose-frosted cookies.

"Well, she looks happy, at least," Winnie said. "I guess it must work for people here!"

"Yeah. Uh. I guess."

Ahmad leaned in closer, trying to catch the woman's eye. She continued to slap the side of her sifter, eyes cast downward.

"Ahmad! Come on! We don't have time."

Winnie tugged him onward, and Ahmad could hear the crackle of electricity behind him as the shop shifted again. A shiver crept down his spine. Was Winnie right? Was the lady fine with knowing that if someone didn't want to buy from her, the store would somehow snap her out of existence until she was wanted again?

"Let's get back to Madame Nasirah's before it disappears," Winnie said as they paused on a street corner. Pedestrians waited on one side of a wide crevasse, through which they could see down into more neon blue, bustling areas of Paheli. Ahmad's stomach lurched. It was hard to get used to them. "Something tells me crossing the street here isn't as easy as it is in Manhattan, and besides, we need to review what we learned," she added.

"You're right."

It took a few stops and flickers, but Winnie and Ahmad finally shuffled back into the tea shop, decidedly worse for the wear. Madame Nasirah stared at them blankly for a moment, as if she'd already forgotten—again—who they were. But then she looked down at the knapsacks in her hands with a start and smiled.

"You're just in time," she said. "I've prepared your

bags." She handed one to each of them, and looked up expectantly, awaiting their response to the goodies she'd shared.

Ahmad unzipped the knapsack that Madame Nasirah had given him. She had loaded it, along with Winnie's, with handfuls of small tools and treats, holding them up and naming them as she went.

"Map. A water bottle. A lantern. Believe me, you'll want to keep track of that. And . . . oh my!"

Crash!

Both of them nearly jumped out of their skin when a huge sword clattered out of the woman's hand, missing Madame Nasirah's foot in favor of spearing the wooden floor.

Madame Nasirah had stared down and, after a moment, shrugged complacently. "Well, just in case." She tucked it away in Ahmad's knapsack and gave the stuffed bag a reassuring pat.

Now he squirmed against the wall as Winnie examined everything they were given.

"I really hope this isn't an RPG," she moaned.

"Me too," Ahmad said fervently. He hated open world RPGs more than any other type of video game.

The idea of spending all that time exploring, fumbling through side quests and debating which ones were actually worthwhile to accomplishing the goals of the storyline, was utterly stressful. What if you chose wrong? What if you missed that right turn on the road that would lead to a good ending? It just made him antsy.

As he continued to dig, he came upon the final layer at the bottom of the bag: sandwiches of fresh falafel stuffed into warm pita pockets, Ahmad's favorite mithai, chenna murki, and sweet qatayef dumplings filled with nuts and drizzled with honey. But before he could comment on the thoughtful provisions, a sudden hush descended upon the shop, as though a large hand had reached down and cupped itself about the electric nerves and twitching veins of the great, sprawling city.

Had Paheli frozen like New York City, another glitch in the game? The kids looked at each other nervously, but Madame Nasirah had only hummed to herself meditatively.

"Wait just a moment. It will be over shortly."

There was a distant clatter. And then, abruptly, there was a fizz and whizz of air, like someone had let off fireworks. Ahmad and Winnie both rushed for the window and the metal shutters before it gave way, just enough for them to see a flare of green light spark up from the tip of the minaret at the very heart of the city. The light ebbed down into small veins set into the sides of the structure, making the entire building grow.

"That's the signal," Madame Nasirah said behind them. "When the Minaret flares, one of the challenges of the game begins. It can be seen from anywhere in the city. Consider it the beating heart of Paheli."

"It's beautiful," breathed Winnie, pressing her hand against the shutters.

"I know," Ahmad responded quietly. He absently rubbed his hand against his chest. Something about the Minaret, even in his sketches, reached inside and scratched its nails over old scars in his heart in the worst sort of way. It brought up memories of pain and panic without him even being able to identify what those memories were.

He yelped, jumping back, as something pelted against the window from the inside—right near where he rested his fingers.

"What was that?" Winnie asked, her eyes wide.

Ahmad slowly knelt to pick up the objects. As his fingers glided over them, words sparked in the air.

OBTAINED: BOAT!

OBTAINED: NET!

"Are these . . . some sort of tokens?" Winnie held up her object—the small net—to the light. "Oh wow. It's so detailed!"

Ahmad leaned in over her shoulder and narrowed his eyes. It was incredibly delicate, as though it had been knitted on the tiniest needles possible. Winnie was right: Every stitch, once you leaned in, was obvious and etched out with care. It trembled against her fingertips under the softness of their breath.

"Do we exchange these for the real things?" Ahmad asked Madame Nasirah, who just shook her head. "I cannot give you details on how to use them. I just make sure you receive them."

"Typical," Ahmad muttered under his breath. It was a very adult thing to say: *You need to figure it out on your own.* But what if you never seemed to do that properly? He turned his attention back to the boat. It was as intricately crafted as the net.

"What kind of boat is that?" Winnie asked, leaning in over his shoulder.

"Oh. Um." Ahmad's tongue stumbled. He knew this type of boat. He did. Well, not really, but he'd seen it in the picture books his father brought home from trips to Bangladesh when he was younger. "Oh! A dinghy! It's a type of rowboat. I think."

Both Ahmad and Winnie startled when a sudden shower of fireworks cartwheeled through the sky. In their wake, they left glittering words. TRIAL: RESCUE THE MACHI MEN FROM DROWNING IN THE DEPTHS OF PAHELI'S GREAT RIVER!

"What is that?" Winnie asked, but Ahmad was already opening the door and rushing outside of the shop to crane his head up toward the sky.

Beneath the shimmering letters, a countdown clock burst into existence: big red numbers blazing against their eyes. Thirty minutes spiraled backward.

"Wait, wait, wait!" Ahmad gasped. "The countdown starts now?"

"Machi Men," Winnie said dazedly as the words faded away. "What could that even mean? Machine men?"

"Machi . . . ," Ahmad said slowly, turning the boat he still held over in his fingers. "That also means 'fish' in Hindu and Urdu." For once, his brain wasn't failing him on the right word, but the rest left him at a loss. Since when did Paheli have a river? And how could fish-men, if he was actually right, drown?

"I don't understand." Winnie shook her head. "None of this feels remotely like a normal game. This is not strategy. This is not teamwork. This is us being told to save some people or else they drown! How can the Architect do this?"

As though in response to her question, the door thumped closed behind them. They turned to see Madame Nasirah cheerfully waving out the window and pointing toward the ground. Their knapsacks rested against the threshold, neatly zipped up.

"Great," Ahmad muttered, staring at it. "I guess giving us another cup of tea before we face our doom was too much to ask."

"I thought you were the one who said not to expect much from adults," Winnie said sharply, but when Ahmad glanced at her face, she had a weakly teasing smile.

"I did, but—" Ahmad muttered. That was before he got used to warmth and comfort and a hand on his shoulder. That was before it really sank in that they were playing a game where the stakes were higher than making the top scores leaderboard or winning valuable, limited-edition armor off another player.

Winnie sighed. "There's nothing else we can do now but try to find that river."

So there they were, ducking down side streets and inching through alleyways. It felt like it had been hours, and there was no sign of water.

There was so much else to take in, though, that it was easy to get distracted. They were definitely in the heart of the souk. Everywhere around were the most lavish things imaginable on sale.

"We should probably stick together," Winnie rushed out as a gaggle of beaming, excitedly chattering women nearly swept them apart. "It's really crowded here and I—Ahmad?"

Ahmad's attention had snagged on a shop window.

"No way," he breathed, plastering his face against it to watch as a salesperson cheerfully waved at a watching family before stepping through a shimmering portal—and reappearing a few feet away, deeper in the shop. "Is that a teleportation device? Do those things really exist?"

"Ahmad," Winnie huffed, striding over to him. "We're supposed to be finding that challenge. Okay? Not window shopping."

Ahmad was entirely engrossed in the wares on display.

"This stuff looks like it could belong in Wakanda! That's some sort of robot assistant. Or maybe it's an android!"

It certainly looked human enough. Apart from the visible blue veins shooting down its cheeks and the slight stilted motion of its body as it shuffled through a demonstration of how it could set a dinner table, there was nothing else to distinguish it from the people eagerly clustered around it.

"Ahmad! Ahmad!" Winnie whirled him around by the shoulder, frowning. "You need to focus. On me." He was still craning his head to see past her.

"Come on, just one more minute," he said distractedly. "It's not like I could find a store like this in New York City."

"Exactly," Winnie snapped. "You couldn't. Because this isn't our world. Listen to me, Ahmad. We promised each other to work together, right?"

Her eyes were wide and worried. Ahmad felt a twinge of remorse. She was right.

"Yeah. I know. Sorry."

She nodded and cleared her throat. "Me too. I got a little intense. Come on, let's keep going."

With one last longing look at the shop of magical wares, Ahmad followed after her.

"I don't understand," Winnie grumbled. "I know they don't want us to win this game, but isn't this too far?"

"My legs ache," Ahmad groaned. His brain buzzed like it was tuned in to the wrong radio channel, too. He tried hard to focus and remember his maps, or at least conjure up one of those dream-snatches that were so clear that he could feel the cobblestones beneath his feet. But it wouldn't give him anything.

It didn't help that after a while, everything started to look the same. Every seller had the same beaming smile and the people who milled about—examining fresh fish and exclaiming over warm bread fresh off a conveyor belt looping around a small bakery stall—all melted into one another.

They'd been walking for what felt like hours, but it didn't seem like they'd even left the shopping district yet. How could that be? And where was this challenge?

He flopped down against a street corner in frustration and groped in his bag for his little packet of treats. "I need a snack break."

Winnie barely heard him, tapping absently against the stone beneath her feet. "That map is useless," she announced. "It has no compass rose, and just squiggly lines for the streets. It just looks like a rat maze."

"*The water is coming*," an eerie voice whispered.

Ahmad looked up from a packet of chenna murki, about to ask Winnie why she sounded like that, and froze.

"What is that?"

"Come on, Ahmad." Even with her back turned, it was obvious Winnie was rolling her eyes. "Even if you don't believe it, I know you better than our teachers do."

"Winnie," Ahmad hissed.

"So don't try to put on that tough bad boy act and

tell me you don't know what a compass rose is. Don't accept the label they put on you."

"Winnie!"

Winnie whirled around. "Ahmad, I'm *trying* to give you a compliment. . . ."

She froze as well.

Because standing in front of a trembling Ahmad was a huge, six-foot-tall mouse, dressed as though it was preparing for a presentation of *The Nutcracker*.

Ahmad tried to inch backward, but the mouse only had eyes for the open packet of chenna murki he held in his hands. As Winnie finally snapped into action and hurtled forward, the mouse snatched the bag of sweets out of his fingers and bolted down an alleyway.

"Hey!" Ahmad hollered after it.

Winnie shuddered, rubbing her hands down her arms. "Ugh, ugh, ugh," she said. "I didn't sign up for *Rodents of Unusual Size*. And I thought the rats you see in Times Square were huge."

Then she backed up with a gasp, grasping Ahmad's arm, as the mouse reappeared, not a foot away from where they stood, moving lightly on its haunches and peering at them with bright brown eyes.

The kids held on to each other and stared.

"Um," the mouse said.

Winnie squealed again and seized Ahmad's arm.

"Did the giant rat just talk? To us?" Winnie asked. "Is this part of you being the chosen one of this world or whatever?"

"Who said I was the chosen one of anything?" Ahmad hissed back. "And believe me, if giant talking rodents were any part of my Paheli, I would have mentioned it by now."

"I would prefer T.T. to giant talking rat, if you don't mind," the mouse said primly. It still held the open packet of chenna murki between its paws. "And I'm a mouse, not a rat. I think. Apologies for scaring you. I just wanted to warn you. The water is coming."

"What do you mean?"

The mouse started to count.

"One . . .

Two . . .

Three . . ."

The sky, which had already been dark—but, at least, a comforting dark, broken through with the distant twinkling stars of occupied apartment windows—was now ominous, curdled with seething clouds and occasional claps of lightning.

Water seeped from the ground beneath their feet. It lapped about Winnie's ankles and she danced from foot to foot with a shudder. "Ahmad? What's going on now?"

Ahmad couldn't answer her, but a familiar feeling coiled in his spine.

Dread.

And then the river broke free around them.

CHAPTER EIGHT

AHMAD HAD TAKEN HIS first swimming lessons in Bangladesh. They were not the eased-in, water wing–inclusive fare of the local city pool. One of his cousins had simply tossed him in. But rather than sinking like a stone, it was as though the river itself had risen to embrace him, welcoming him back into his heritage along with the silvery fish that darted between his toes and the petals tangled in his hair when he resurfaced to his family's giddy congratulations.

This water was different. It hit Ahmad hard, every drop feeling like shards of cold, sharp glass. He groped in the inky dark, relieved when he felt Winnie's hand grasp his, and tore against the current until they broke the surface.

He sputtered out a mouthful of river.

"This way," T.T. the mouse called, paddling ahead of them. Were mice always such adept swimmers?

A dock had emerged over what was previously a street and now was overflowing with water.

By the time Ahmad and Winnie worked their way onto the lip of the deck, they were exhausted. They sloshed and skidded back and forth on the wet wood, holding each other for balance as they gingerly picked their way forward.

"Giving us some rain boots would have been a good idea!" Ahmad hollered over the wailing wind. "Or maybe some of those sticky cup things to put underneath our shoes."

"I'm not sure if those would actually help in this weather," Winnie called back. "At least we now know how life feels when you are a stick of butter."

"Did we actually need to know that, though?" Ahmad shouted back, but the winds swallowed his words.

Ahmad squinted upward. Through the damp in his eyes, he could just make out the glowing Minaret. That awful red timer was still there too, broadcast over the horizon with all the subtlety of the Bat Signal. Five minutes.

Ahmad exclaimed, "Five minutes? Really? After dumping us into that without warning?"

He reached into the soggy depths of his knapsack.

"Useless, useless, useless," chanted Winnie as he sorted through the mess of items, surfacing first with the sodden bag of food and then with the map, bleeding ink all over his fingers. "Is that really all of it?"

"This is ridiculous," Ahmad seethed, water dripping off his eyelashes. No, it was more than that. It was just like school. You were told what to do, but never given what you needed to do it. You were told that you needed to try harder, but the game was already rigged in someone else's favor.

Angrily he dumped the knapsack out on the dock. Something clattered against the slick wood, and Ahmad picked it up. It was the miniature boat. He stared at it, and then at Winnie.

"This could be a red herring," she said cautiously.

"But remember the token? And my Switch screen?" Ahmad lifted the boat over the churning water. T.T., who had been mumbling to himself and wringing out his damp paws, noticed the movement and his eyes widened.

"No! You can't! Not so close to the dock!"

But Ahmad had already dropped it.

"Oops."

Winnie sighed and opened her mouth, but then let out a shriek instead.

"What—what is it doing?"

The water shifted and sloshed against the dock. Ahmad and Winnie braced themselves against each other.

"Oh my gosh!" Winnie gasped.

"Ugh!" Ahmad spluttered as a huge wave splashed into his mouth, carrying the awful taste of brackish water and thick sludge.

With a final buck and a heave, the tiny boat billowed out into the river, becoming large enough to seat two kids and a very, very large mouse. It was definitely one of the dinghies from Ahmad's childhood picture books, resembling a regular rowboat, but with elegant carvings and bright flowers blooming on its sides.

"Uh, wow," Ahmad said, at a loss for any other words.

"I'm not going to get used to this," Winnie said dazedly.

Ahmad tugged her onto the craft. T.T. took hold of the oars and they jetted away over the river's surface.

The kids craned their necks to see into the water, white-capped waves surging forward against the bow of the boat. Even as a city kid, Ahmad could tell that current was strong.

"Nothing yet," Ahmad muttered.

"We don't even know what we're looking for," Winnie pointed out. "Where are these Machi Men? *Who* are these Machi Men? And how do we get them?"

She shrieked as their boat suddenly tilted to the side. Something had bumped into it, hard. Ahmad leaned over the side, his heart pounding. Giant fingers were curling up from beneath the boat.

"What is that?"

The fingers curled over the side of the boat. There was another moment, breaking the water's surface: a giant, metallic face.

A Machi Man. And though it was carved and not at all human, it looked like it was pleading.

Winnie jumped back, frightened by the shimmery,

scaly fish-man, and nearly took Ahmad down with her as she toppled.

The Machi Man's metallic grasp slipped.

"Winnie! We need to catch him!" Ahmad bolted forward, Winnie behind him, and the two kids tried to catch hold of one of the slippery fingers, but it slid through their hands. The Machi Man glided back into the water as they tumbled to the floor of the boat.

Righting themselves, they pondered their predicament, peering over the edge of the boat to spy a fleet of fish-men statues sinking quickly into the depths of the water.

"Great." Winnie gritted through her teeth. "They are huge. I guess trying to help them out is what the net is for, then."

In the water below, a good half dozen Machi Men floated aimlessly in the water, frozen fingers waving as they were tugged down by the current. Ahmad and Winnie tossed out the net again and again, but every time they managed to drag them upward, the boat nearly capsized. Trying to grasp their huge hands didn't work. The Machi Men were too slippery and too heavy.

"This is not going to work," Ahmad gasped out, trying to steady himself in the wildly rocking boat.

"We need to do something," Winnie yelled back. "The timer's showing only minutes left!"

But what?

These Machi Men were built like anchors, heavy and solid, and their sinking seemed inevitable. What could they use to propel them back up out of the water and into the boat, where they belonged?

They were running out of time.

And fast.

"Think, think, think," Ahmad chanted to himself. His hand dangled over the side of the boat.

Something lurched upward out of the water and grasped Ahmad's wrist. He yelped.

"Winnie! Help me!"

"Ahmad!" Winnie rushed to his side and gasped. "What is that?"

"I . . . don't know . . . but it won't let go! Ugh!" Ahmad shook his wrist in vain. Was it some sort of water ghoul? The Paheli of his daydreams had never been this violent or cruel, but now it seemed to be pulling out the stops. He hated it.

"Okay, okay, change of plans," Winnie rushed out, before grasping him around the waist. "If we can't make it let go of you, we haul it out and kick some butt to make it sorry it dared to."

"Wait, what?"

But Winnie was already tugging.

"T.T., I could use a little help here!"

"Oh, right!" T.T. scrambled behind her, resting a paw on Ahmad's side. Ahmad shuddered. Even through layers of soggy clothing he could feel barely sheathed claws, and it was almost as uncomfortable as the clammy thing around his wrist.

"Heave-ho!" Winnie hollered, and she and T.T. tugged while Ahmad threw himself backward. As he stumbled to the deck, whatever had been holding him broke free of the water's surface and landed in the boat with a hard thud.

"Ouch, ouch, ouch," a husky voice said from the bottom of the boat. "Oh, that was a mistake. That hurts."

Ahmad rubbed his wrist and stared hard at the sodden mass on the floor.

"That voice. It sounds familiar."

"What?" Winnie asked, but before she could do anything else, Ahmad was already stumbling forward. "Ahmad, be careful! We don't know what that is."

"I think I do," Ahmad panted. It was definitely a human body: tall and lanky, with a damp thatch of hair that a skinny hand was brushing back. Underneath was a face he knew all too well, and a weary smile that still managed to be mischievous.

"What are you doing here?" Ahmad demanded, even as he couldn't help but return a very astonished smile of his own.

Of all the people in the world he could have expected to see, here and now, his uncle wasn't one of them.

But there he was, in the flesh.

Vijay Bhai cleared his throat. "I'm here to help you," he announced, raising an arm. "Now, who's going to help me up?"

CHAPTER NINE

IN TIMES OF TROUBLE, Ahmad had his own rituals to ground himself and keep his stomach from tying itself into knots and his knees from shaking: holding his Switch under the table during a difficult test, or popping a few chenna murki into his mouth and letting them melt into his tongue.

They weren't meant to hold off the trouble he would inevitably get into, and they never did. But at least, while he focused on them, his brain had a chance to get itself into gear and maybe find a solution for him.

Now he stuck his hand into his pocket. It was a habit from when he was a little kid. But the marbles he was reaching for had been lost years ago. He wished he had them now, as he watched Vijay Bhai wring his hair out between his hands like a washcloth.

"Oh, that's cold." Vijay Bhai winced as water seeped between his fingers.

"Uh, Ahmad?" Winnie said slowly. "Who is this?"

"My uncle," Ahmad responded. "Well, more or less."

To be entirely accurate, Vijay Bhai was his aunt's best friend. It was kind of weird, because he just didn't seem the type to be friends with Aunt Zohra. She was tall, lanky, and awkward, and he was tall, lanky, and young. That was weird too.

He never seemed the right age to properly be an uncle, mentally or physically.

Winnie was still staring at him, and Ahmad looked at Vijay Bhai through her eyes: the shiny gold hoop through his right ear, thanks to a recent Piercing Pagoda adventure, the light dusting of a beard over his jaw, and that wide, wide grin—even though they had just fished him out of a river in a whole other world.

"Nice to know Paheli is as welcoming as it always was," Vijay Bhai said with a wink in Ahmad's direction. He reached out and rumpled Ahmad's hair with clammy fingers. "And I'm really glad to see you're in one piece. When I saw how things changed, I was starting to get worried about how I'd find you. I got a little lost, too. Thought I knew this place like I made it up myself."

"You know Paheli too?" Winnie blurted out, at the same time Ahmad gasped, "You knew we were here? But . . . our world is frozen!"

Vijay Bhai nodded. Droplets of water skied down the bridge of his nose. "I know. I was taking a walk around the block—well, honestly, I was at your house and your mom chased me out with the broom again so she could cook without me underfoot—and the entire world came to a halt."

"But not you," Winnie interjected.

"No. And because of that, I was able to put together the puzzle pieces of what was happening." Vijay Bhai's face was abruptly solemn. "It's happened to me once before, you know."

"What—" Ahmad sputtered. His mind was reeling. Vijay Bhai was still talking, though.

"But we don't have time for all that. Not now. I think I have something you might need."

He reached out, dropping something into Ahmad's still-wet palm.

Ahmad started when his hand felt something round, smooth, and cold settle into it.

OBTAINED! Text flashed before his eyes in a bright gold, holographic font. The words looked almost as solid as whatever was in his hand. MARBLE!

"A marble?" Ahmad whispered to himself. His heart pounded.

He held it up. It was the usual clear sphere, with a winking core of bright green. It rolled over his palm, catching light in spite of the brooding darkness closing in around them.

"This can't be one of mine," Ahmad mumbled, staring down at it. Marbles were pretty much the same everywhere, right? Besides, Ma had probably dumped his own precious collection into the nearest Goodwill collection box as soon as he got bored of them back in fifth grade.

Any marble could look like this, as clear and calm as a cat's eye. Any marble could have the familiar scratches from the grooves of the Queens sidewalk he still remembered bouncing over on his way to kindergarten.

This wasn't one of his marbles. And yet, here it was, in a moment when he needed its reassuring coolness most. That couldn't be a coincidence.

Vijay Bhai stared at him calmly. "Try it, Ahmad," he said quietly. "You can't win this game unless you take chances."

"These clouds worry me," Winnie called from behind him. "We need to figure this out fast!"

"Hold on a moment!" Ahmad yelled back, cupping the marble in his hands as the moisture made his palms slippery. He needed to keep a good grip on it so he could think.

The rest of the equipment that Madame Nasirah had tucked into their satchels was proving to be useless in this challenge. But what if the marble *was* also part of that equipment? Was this what they were looking for?

"Winnie, I think I've got something!"

Winnie sloshed toward him, tossing out her arms to balance on the swaying deck. "What is it? What did you get?"

She squinted at the marble in his hand.

"A marble?" she asked. "How can that possibly help? These are giants, Ahmad."

"It's magnetic. I used to collect marbles when I was a kid. I'm sure of it. These guys are giants, but they are metal giants. This is the key, Winnie. I can feel it."

Winnie's brow was furrowed doubtfully. "Okay. I get that. But I'm not sure how something so small could be used to fish out those huge men."

She glanced at Vijay Bhai, who had moved from his hair to wringing out his sleeve, and leaned in closer to whisper, "Also, you really need to explain this whole uncle but not an uncle thing to me."

Ahmad nodded. It was a fair point, about fishing out the men, and one he hadn't figured out yet—not that he could explain the whole Vijay thing either. He closed his hands over the marble and rubbed them together, feeling the marble slide over his skin. And then, he closed his eyes, too.

"Grow," he whispered. "Please. Grow."

"Uh, Ahmad . . . ," Winnie began, and then gasped as the marble rolled out from between Ahmad's fingers.

"No!" Ahmad cried, and reached out for it, but it toppled off the deck and into the water, without even a splash.

"So much for that," Winnie sighed. "Sorry, Ahmad."

Ahmad stared mournfully into the water. "It felt like we were on the right track," he whispered.

The boat began to tremble, listing from side to side. Winnie and Ahmad grasped each other's arms, and Ahmad felt Vijay Bhai grasp the back of his shirt.

"Steady," Vijay Bhai warned.

"I think something is under the boat!" Winnie shouted.

The Machi Men, in a panic, were thrashing back and forth. The kids clung to each other as the water seethed around their small craft.

"We have to do something," Winnie said angrily. "We can't let them down like this."

"But what else can we do? We've tried everything we were given."

"Not everything . . . we could . . ." Ahmad frantically reached for his knapsack, tugging out the bag of food.

"That's not going to do anything, Ahmad!"

"We don't know that!" Ahmad flung out a soggy pita over the water. It sank. He tossed another.

"Ahmad. Ahmad, stop."

Winnie grasped his arm, and then her jaw hung as

she saw why Ahmad had actually stopped. The bread was growing, spreading out over the water like a flotation device—or maybe a very brown, very soggy piece of paper towel. As the water receded, there was something silvery and round and very large in its depths.

"The marble," Ahmad whispered. "It is magnetic."

The Machi Men clung to it, and Ahmad and Winnie watched as metallic lips turned upward and unhinged jaws clacked together happily.

"It's working, it's working!" Winnie squealed, tapping Ahmad's arm excitedly.

As soon as the last Machi Man was attached to the marble, it started rolling toward the boat. Ahmad's and Winnie's joy died quickly.

"That thing is going to crash into the side of the boat, *Titanic*-style!" Winnie shrieked.

Ahmad was already drawing down his hoodie, letting the water spatter against his bare head.

"Ahmad, what are you *doing*?" Winnie demanded.

"Winnie, I need you to grab hold of my legs and pull me back into the boat once I've been able to touch the marble and make it shrink back again," Ahmad said calmly, rolling up his sleeves.

"Are you serious? Ahmad, that water is churning! It'll just sweep you away!"

"It's that or we pull the marble aboard and let the boat sink with the weight of it," Ahmad pointed out. "I'll be fine. Can I trust you to keep a firm grip?"

"I'll hold on to the oars," Vijay Bhai added from behind them. "Along with your"—he peered at T.T. and the mouse gave him an anxious look—"other friend."

Winnie stared hard at Ahmad and then sighed.

"Of course I won't let go of you."

"I know you won't. So we're both good," Ahmad said, smiling.

He took a deep breath and leaned over the side of the boat, waiting until he could feel Winnie get a grip on his legs. He reached out, farther and farther. He could see the reflection of his face in the marble's shiny surface. If he could just stretch out his fingers . . .

"Thank you for your service," he grunted, reaching out, "but I'm going to need you to . . . shrink!"

His fingers connected. Beneath them, the marble shrank, tumbling for the water. He made a final lunge and caught it between his hands, complete with the mini Machi Men attached to its sides.

"I've got it!" he crowed. His joy was short-lived as he realized he was teetering for balance.

"Ahmad!" Winnie cried, but he was already under-water. The river ran into his mouth, weirdly briny in a way that reminded him of pickles. He choked and sputtered and gasped for air. His lungs felt like there were pins and needles jabbing into them. Was this what it felt like to drown?

He tried to focus on keeping the marble between his fingers, but he could hardly feel his fingers from the shock and sting of the cold water.

After a few seconds he was yanked upward, gasping and coughing, back into the boat.

"I can't believe you," Winnie scolded him, anxiously patting him on the shoulders. "That was the bravest and most ridiculous thing I've ever seen someone do in my life. Boys, I tell you."

But Ahmad was only focused on his hands. "I lost it," he chanted unhappily. "I lost it, I lost it, I lost . . . no, I didn't lose it!"

He held up the marble triumphantly. The metallic, now miniature Machi Men attached to its sides waved their arms and hands.

Grinning widely, Winnie and Ahmad waved back.

"We did it, Winnie," Ahmad said, sniffling.

Winnie laughed. "Now to get you dried off!"

But before they could make another move, the water abruptly slid away from the ship, receding so that they could see—once again—the long dock and alleyways of the shore.

And, hovering dramatically, without a hair out of place or a droplet on her sleeve, was the MasterMind.

CHAPTER TEN

W

ELL DONE, CHAMPIONS!" THE MasterMind said, extending both arms forward toward Winnie and Ahmad with a gleeful smile on her face.

She was floating on a decked-out hoverboard, framed on every side with incredible blasters and iridescent lights. Standing there like that, she looked she was trying to be a jovial uncle at Eid, the type that pinched your cheek and smacked your back and stuffed a sweet in your mouth while pressing money in your hand.

She totally failed. Particularly since no uncle Ahmad knew, even the ones with questionable taste, ever wore zebra-print leggings with a rainbow T-shirt that had "Bad things come in small packages" across the front. She was also wearing one of those bucket hats he usually saw sweet grandmas in Chinatown wearing on really sunny days.

"Who is this clown?" Vijay Bhai muttered out of the side of his mouth.

Ahmad sighed. "Our worst nightmare."

Vijay Bhai gave a low chuckle. "I've seen worse."

Winnie crossed her arms over her chest. She would have looked intimidating if it wasn't for her soaked hair and flushed face. "You seem like you enjoyed all that trouble you caused it."

The MasterMind smirked. "You're right. I do."

She stepped elegantly forward, and with every footfall, the water seemed to cringe back from direct contact with so much as the tip of her boots. Even it was nervous around her. Ahmad swallowed hard.

"You're supposed to entertain us, and though that was a nice appetizer, I feel we can do better during the next round," the MasterMind said. "Of course, now the training wheels are off. I didn't work my fingers to the bone for you guys to traipse around all sweetness and light and occasional tea breaks."

"This was sweetness and light?" Winnie hollered indignantly.

The MasterMind put her hand on her hip and smirked. "Those Machi Men could have stood a few more kilos in the shins. You're welcome."

Winnie's skin was starting to work its way toward an angry flush, so Ahmad stepped in front, crossing his arms in solidarity with his bedraggled classmate.

"If you're going to give us a villain monologue, at least make it useful," he said. "So we've finished this level. What's next? Don't we get a cool rundown of stats in the sky and things we've earned? A grumpy Moogle to haggle with over health potions and speed boosters?"

"I thought you'd never ask." The MasterMind lifted her hand and snapped her fingers. Lightning crackled across the static sky and then, in large yellow letters, words flashed.

TUTORIAL COMPLETE!

BONUS TIME—0:05

"You may want to step out of the way for this one if you plan to keep going," the MasterMind warned.

Ahmad puzzled over that, but Winnie's eyes widened and she grasped his arm. "Duck!"

She tugged him out of the way moments before a large sack of coins nailed the spot he'd stood in moments before. It was only another second before other items followed: an oversized, jingling set of keys that flickered for a moment, exposing bright pixels and silver current, a snaking mess of cables, what looked to be a CD case that shattered as it hit the ground, and a large puzzle piece like the one Madame Nasirah had shown them before.

Ahmad and Winnie stared at the pile, as above it, the letters giddily spun and jostled each other to reveal:

REWARDS!

X1 Keys

X1 Cables

X1 Duff Drum Collection CD

"What is all this?" Winnie asked. "Do we really need all this for the next challenge?"

The MasterMind gave another one of those irksome smirks. "I got bored with that CD. You're welcome."

Vijay Bhai knelt and gathered up the shattered

jewel case. "That was a classic," he muttered angrily. "Kids these days."

Ahmad couldn't pay attention, though. He grabbed Winnie by the arm as new holographic words flashed in the air before them: YOU'VE EARNED A PUZZLE PIECE! ONLY—the letters faded into static for a moment—TO GO!

For a moment, the MasterMind's triumphant expression fell.

"It wasn't supposed to do that," she muttered. Her hoverboard lowered, and she waved a hand toward the letters so that they faded.

"Well, there you go," she said as Winnie fell to her knees and reverently gathered up the puzzle piece. She flashed it at Ahmad, who gasped.

It was larger than he expected and didn't look like what he imagined when he thought of a puzzle piece at all, or even the example that Madame Nasirah had conjured up for them. It was marble-carved, shaped like a monkey's head with the eye of the animal formed by an inlaid stone.

"Hey, um, do we get a user's manual along with this?" demanded Winnie, spinning around to face the

MasterMind. But the girl, hoverboard under her arm, was already halfway into what appeared to be another flying car—one that was definitely a Ferrari compared to the rickety rickshaw model they had briefly used— sleek and stunning with a silver sheen.

"Good luck! You'll need all you can get!" she called, and then the little craft zoomed off.

Great. Just great.

"Now what?" Ahmad demanded impatiently, but Winnie seized his arm.

"Um, Ahmad?"

"What is it?"

He looked up.

"Oh," he said weakly. "Great."

Their mouse friend was back. And he brought company with him: a whole lot of his kin.

"Oh gosh," Winnie said weakly as the mice gathered about them, jostling and rolling their eyes at one another and smoothing their whiskers. "This is my mom's worst nightmare. Not mine, though," she added hastily as one stepped closer. "I like mice."

"How do you feel about lizards?" Vijay Bhai asked cheerfully. If it had been any other moment, Ahmad would have shot him a glare. *Not the time.*

"Okay, okay, back up. Let's not crowd the future champions!" To Ahmad and Winnie's relief, T.T. brushed through the crowd and rushed up to them.

"Sorry, but can you pick up the pace?" T.T. said shrilly. "Look, you guys need to focus. I don't know what the MasterMind told you, but I assure you she's downplaying her own talent to keep you underestimating her—and you should never underestimate a girl."

Winnie nodded in agreement.

"The Architect is a spoiled brat, bloated on his own power and used to doing the bare minimum to keep it. The MasterMind is pampered and proud, but has a nice set of teeth she keeps hidden. If you tempt her, she'll turn on you and bite. Hard."

"We know," Ahmad broke in. "We've been keeping track of time too."

T.T. raised a furry brow and pointed up at the sky. Ahmad and Winnie craned their heads up. Right on the borderline of the sky underneath a pixelated crescent was the countdown clock, its numbers churning back so rapidly that Ahmad could hardly make out what time it was.

Ahmad groaned.

"Great. I can hardly make it through a quiz at school in one period and now we have to be timed on this."

"Okay, but you *do* finish it," Winnie pointed out. "Just like you finish games. You're with me, too, remember? I'm always the first person finished."

"No need to brag about it," Ahmad muttered. He knew that very well. The sight of her prim head bent happily over a book as he continued to labor through a state test was familiar, and always gave him that same sting of resentment.

"And we're going to help you," T.T. chimed in. "Consider us your cheering squad. We're new to the job, certainly, but that gives us character!"

"New to the job?" Winnie asked.

"Paheli didn't really . . . welcome residents of our nature in the past," one of the mice said sheepishly. "The fact that we're here now is only because so many updates, upgrades, and upheavals have worn tunnels through the city's fortifications."

"Meaning," another mouse said pertly, "that under all the fluff and fancy cars, Paheli is rotting. And the

Architect can't do as much about it as he used to."

Before Ahmad could begin to reply, the mice were nudging them along to the steering. They paused, though, and turned expectantly toward Ahmad. They stared. He stared back.

"Oh." He reached into his bag. Ahmad passed out chenna murki to much excited squeaking and thanks. But he worried that he would run out quick, and wondered if the sweet snack was all that would keep these squeaky sidekicks on Team Ahmad and Winnie.

"All right, go ahead and steer," T.T. said.

Ahmad hesitated, before jumping nearly out of his skin as the sky lit up. It took a moment for him to realize what they were seeing were projected images of what was happening elsewhere in the city: both cities, the one that lived and the one that waited, frozen, for their triumphant return. It was like a wider, brighter—and well, sadder—version of the Bat Signal.

New York was still, even as the dying sun cast golden light over the buildings and frozen inhabitants. Paheli, though it bustled and hummed with raised voices and moving feet, was almost frantic to prove that it was still alive. People cast their eyes about and hurried on.

Merchants' calls for business echoed with desperation.

Ahmad clenched his jaw, as Vijay Bhai settled in behind him and Winnie turned on the boat.

"Full speed ahead, for our city and our families!" she called out.

And off they went.

CHAPTER ELEVEN

AHMAD WASN'T A BIG fan of going fast and without brakes.

Winnie, though, decidedly was.

"All right!" she cheered, plowing the boat through a chain of golden coins floating in air as they jetted over the river. "Another ten points!"

Since it was on their route and not a deterrence to where they needed to go—or where they thought they needed to go, anyway—Winnie was determined to win. Every obstacle she managed to drag the boat through or flung by with a narrow yank on the wheel showered the floor with gold coins.

By the time they had churned to sweet stillness, Ahmad was queasy and staggered out of the boat, barely taking note of Winnie's disappointment.

"The coins turned into trading cards of the Architect!" She fanned them out, scowling at them as the images smirked and preened. Ahmad glanced briefly. The boy depicted on them was more or less his age, but also older in a way. Perhaps it was the bottomless dark of his eyes, or the bruise-like circles around them.

Ahmad shuddered and looked away.

"Let's give Ahmad a moment to breathe," T.T. chirruped as he bounded out of the back of the boat. "It is odd that the Minaret hasn't flared again, but I suppose the MasterMind and the Architect are cooking up another new trick. We'll have to be ready for it."

"Before we leap straight into strategy, can I call for a first aid field trip?" Winnie held up her finger ruefully. Ahmad hissed in sympathy at the angry red cut across it. "The sharp edges of those Machi Men were no joke!"

T.T. nodded. "Might as well. You can see more of the city, too."

The first stop was one of the main streets, apparently, for shopping: broad with large archways, rooftop gardens spilling over like Rapunzel's hair down buildings where people milled in and out, carrying items under their arms like richly etched teapots and sacks of fine spices.

They found a seller that offered bolts of lush gauze woven by spiders with uncomfortably cunning, human eyes. Apparently, Band-Aids weren't a thing.

"Healthier for you than anything woven or spun elsewhere," the woman chattered cheerfully as Winnie cautiously extended her hand. "You'll hardly see a scar afterward."

"But will the nightmares be worth it?" Ahmad couldn't help but blurt out. Winnie elbowed him in the side.

"Stop it. You're making me nervous."

Ahmad stepped back. He was still haunted by a bad dream from back when he was probably five and six: a horrendous, looming montage of metallic mandibles, sticky webs, and needle-thin legs tapping across stone.

It didn't comfort him at all that the spiders' gaze never left him, even as the one chosen out of those hanging down from the shop's awning carefully wound strands around Winnie's wounded finger.

Vijay Bhai, too, had backed away, whistling tonelessly under his breath as he poked at a screen advertising digitally printed tapestries and customized bedsheets.

Winnie, though, was enchanted.

"This place is incredible," she said in awe. "I wish our spiders at home were this cool."

"I'm glad they aren't," Ahmad interjected. He was relieved when they moved on.

"I don't remember any of this," Vijay Bhai remarked idly as they strode on. "Where are the dollar carts of samosas and the man who sold wishing lamps?"

That reminded Ahmad, and he tugged on his uncle's arm to make him stop. "You never did tell me why you know so much about Paheli."

Vijay Bhai didn't look him in the face, still staring upward toward the plexiglass balconies and digital billboards. "I've spent some time here, in the past."

"Wait, really? As a player? When? How?"

"So does that mean you won the game?" Winnie interjected eagerly.

"Unfortunately, no." Vijay Bhai's mouth twisted bitterly. "My experience . . . well, let's say it was less of a pleasurable trip and more of a forced stay."

"So you were trapped in here?" Ahmad asked. He tried to picture Vijay Bhai surviving in Paheli, and just couldn't see it. To describe Vijay Bhai as bad with technology was an understatement. Even Ma understood what YouTube was, how to log in to her e-mail, and she could definitely tell you about a few popular shows on TV.

Vijay Bhai, though—forget YouTube, he was still wrapping his mind around the Internet, and personal computers. It took him a month to figure out how to hail a taxi, and the smallest excursion, like going to Starbucks or the local library, was treated with the same excitement as a vacation overseas.

Picturing him in this world of floating crosswalks and flying cars was impossible.

"It wasn't anything like this," Vijay Bhai said, waving his arm at their surroundings. "Back then, my best friend and I settled down to play a game that involved sand and simple tokens. We didn't know what we were getting ourselves into. I didn't know how much of my life that one decision would take away from me."

Winnie seemed spellbound. "How much did it take?"

Even T.T., who had gotten distracted by a wide

wheel of cheese suspended in a holographic display case, glanced up at Vijay Bhai to hear his reply.

"Years," Vijay Bhai said softly. "My whole youth, really. And the world moved on without me."

Ahmad was caught by another, small detail. "Your best friend—but wait, wasn't that Aunt Zohra? My aunt Zohra was in here too?"

Vijay Bhai gave him a long, searching look. "You were too young, weren't you?" he said softly, almost as though speaking to himself. "And yet, the memory of Paheli did stay with you in some ways. I should have known, with all the sketchbooks you've filled and the questions you sometimes asked. I should have told you sooner, maybe. I should have been like Zohra and expected it to start again."

Ahmad's mind teemed with questions, and he had no idea where to even begin. Before he could ask more, though, Vijay Bhai briskly clapped his hands together.

"No use for regrets, though. Now we need to make sure this game stops once and for all. You both need to win, and I need to reacquaint myself with Paheli in order to help you. T.T., I don't suppose you know what happened to my balloons after I left here?"

"Balloons?" Winnie asked, confused.

Vijay Bhai smiled. "In my day, I was an aeronaut. The skies of Paheli were my domain and my only friend."

"You—you are the Aeronaut? He is still spoken about!" T.T. squeaked proudly, bowing down a bit, graciously. "Even the new coding couldn't take away Vijay's reputation in Paheli! Unfortunately, though, I think the balloons might have been erased. I don't know for sure, though."

"Is there anyone else from the old game here?" Vijay Bhai asked. "Madame Nasirah, or perhaps Titus Salt, the old man-of-all-trades who kept up the game's mechanisms?"

"We've met Madame Nasirah!" Ahmad said excitedly. "Did you know her, too?"

"Very well," Vijay Bhai said.

T.T.'s whiskers twitched in thought. "You know, I've heard talk that Titus Salt might still haunt one of these alleyways. We haven't seen a lot of him since that MasterMind settled in here, and of course, before she arrived, there wasn't much room or holes for us to wiggle into at all."

"We'll just have to keep an eye out for him as we keep walking," Vijay Bhai decided, and they continued on.

Ahmad remembered some places from his own daydreams, which was a relief. There was a corner of the marketplace devoted to ancient clocks. Not just the European grandfather type, but gold-plated sundials and even a classic water clock from Egypt, featuring a little clay man pouring water between his fingers into a marked barrel on the back of a solemn elephant. As the kids watched, enchanted, the elephant shook its head slowly from side to side.

"That one is more of a display," the seller told them. "Nowadays, these are the best sellers."

He tapped his fingers lightly on a round disk, and they startled backward as holographic numbers scrolled upward toward the sky, bumping into one another before settling down to note the time.

"You can personalize as you wish," the seller continued mildly. "Some of our customers like it peaceful, like this, and others reprogram the numbers to do brief, entertaining presentations as the hour passes."

"If I had a clock like that, I think it would be more distracting than helpful," Winnie hissed to Ahmad.

Most of Paheli's gadgetry seemed to fall under that description: shiny and distracting, but not always in the best way. T.T. made a point of steering them around the waiting cars at the base of the beautiful, glittering funicular rail.

"It doesn't always take you where you need to go," he explained to the wistful kids. "And the last thing we need is to be taken entirely out of the city reaches and have to find our way back."

They wandered down a marbled set of stairs that led up to a rooftop tea shop where Ahmad had absently drawn in small biscuits and abandoned trays of tea on one sketch. It was bigger than he had even imagined though, with an airy balcony holding tables and chairs, and a buffet that held raisin-speckled rice, tender chicken, and individually potted rice puddings. "It just melts in your mouth," mumbled Winnie happily as she sampled the sweets. "This place is better than Disney World."

Ahmad, though, wasn't so sure.

In every store, everyone smiled and had repetitive conversations, pointing at items they apparently had no intention of buying. They lifted empty pots experimentally in their hands and accepted boxes of mithai, and then returned to their previous positions without protest or question.

"No one seems to have a proper home here," Winnie pointed out.

"Or a proper life," Ahmad added, watching as a woman adjusted her scarf for the fifth time in a row.

People drifted into doorways and leaned against the wood grain, looking lost and never venturing inside. They pressed their hands up against the beautiful glass windows, but the shopkeepers looked over their heads in Winnie and Ahmad's direction, their smiles desperate and as sickly sweet as their wares—apparently not aware of their would-be customers' plight, or unable to help even if they were.

"The code doesn't allow for life," T.T. said bitterly. "The MasterMind apparently found it excessive to develop living quarters for creations that are more or less pixels."

"Even if they're programmed, it's so awful!" Ahmad protested. "They look so real, and they look so sad."

He thought of Madame Nasirah, of the desperate hope in her eyes.

As beautiful as Paheli looked, it seemed as though it was just as miserable for its inhabitants as it was for him and Winnie. Determination flowed through him. "We *have* to win this game. We have to change things."

T.T. seemed distracted from the conversation, though, his nose twitching as he examined the buildings.

"There's a lot here I don't recognize, thanks to the last game and the destruction Paheli took from that," T.T. explained. "I don't like to dwell on how the Architect might have achieved it, but he used the MasterMind's ability to code in order to have bodies for souls to be harnessed to."

"So the MasterMind, what's her story?" Vijai Bhai asked, rubbing his chin curiously.

The mouse snarled in disgust. "My memory doesn't go back far enough to settle upon the moment when the Architect allied himself with her," T.T. said. "But it has been a particularly difficult period for the people of Paheli. Familiar landscapes have been tweaked and rearranged to near unrecognition. She toys with all of us, with this world. She's made the city her pet."

Ahmad was distracted for a moment by a group of boys playing a game. They roared and rumbled as they threw down what appeared to be animal knuckles and exchanged cards with sideshow attractions emblazoned on them. One tossed down a card bearing the infamous Sand Shark, another a fierce-looking man chewing off bites from a metal pole.

"Wow," Winnie said. "They look terrifying."

"Ah, yes," T.T. said grimly. "They used to be one of the finest attractions in the district of Lailat. It was a place of eternal night and endless carnivals. But, in spite of all the fun that you could have there, it was still one of the poorest areas of Paheli. It was still disposable."

Vijay Bhai whirled around. "What do you mean disposable?"

"What happened to it?" Ahmad asked tentatively.

T.T. looked away sadly, tugging at his whiskers.

"Another loss for the sake of the city's survival."

Ahmad hadn't even realized how fast Vijay Bhai could move until this moment. He rushed forward, grasping T.T. by the shoulders. T.T. squeaked in alarm.

"Easy, easy, on the fur! And the bones! I'm a delicate creature, you know."

"Please," Vijay Bhai gritted out. "Tell me what

happened to Lailat. That was my home district—as close to a place that belonged to me that this game would ever provide. Where is it now? What did this MasterMind do to Lailat?"

T.T. looked between their anxious faces.

"You know what?" he finally said. "I think it would be best to show you."

CHAPTER TWELVE

T.T. LED THE KIDS and Vijay Bhai down a broad avenue. At first, it looked like all the others they had explored: beautiful shops and kiosks boasting silk scarves that shifted between patterns, or rocket-powered sneakers. But as they continued, it got narrower and narrower.

And that wasn't the only change.

"Why is it getting so dark?" Winnie wondered out loud. "I mean, it's already been dark this whole time."

She was right. There was nothing left of the New York City afternoon they started out with.

"Oh, you haven't seen the true dark yet," T.T. announced ominously. "It surrounds Paheli constantly. Paheli was never a happy city, a proud city, but before it has had its bright moments of hope. It no longer feels that way. Wait just a moment."

Then, as though T.T.'s words had prompted it, the entire sky fell, descending upon them in one abrupt fell swoop.

Winnie shrieked.

Ahmad found himself sucking for air. It felt as though the musty, woolen layers of an unshaken winter blanket were pressing down on him.

The entire sky had collapsed on top of them like a dismantled circus tent. And rather than merely crushing them—pinning them down with shattered poles and weighed fabric—it had managed to work its way into their lungs and was determined to smother every inch possible.

Then it stopped, just as abrupt, as though his futile struggling against nothing but the atmosphere and Winnie's weak whimpers beside him had kicked back the covers.

"That's the last of it," T.T. said, his voice echoing like he was speaking to them through a long tunnel.

"I find that it helps if you keep your eyes closed for a few minutes," he continued. "It won't make a difference in some ways. There's a tenderness behind your lids that won't be shared with the rest of the shadowed world. Take advantage of it for the moment. Breathe."

Ahmad felt calloused, warm fingers clasp his. Winnie. He squeezed two beats—*I'm here*—and felt her squeeze back—*I know*.

They both breathed. Ahmad could hear Vijay Bhai, too, exhaling heavily behind them.

"Wow," he rasped. "I don't remember that from before."

Ahmad could feel the heaviness leaving his lungs. He sucked the air greedily, letting it fill him up like a balloon.

"That suffocation? Remember that feeling," T.T. said. "This is how it will feel if you lose. And now, stick together and hold hands. The path is getting narrower here."

They walked on in silence.

After a few moments, though, Winnie gasped.

"Wait, what is that up ahead?"

There was a gradual but increasing shimmer of light. As they moved toward it, it expanded outward, and by the time they stepped into the middle of it, it was as though they were in a diamond mine.

"Wow," Ahmad gasped, throwing his hand up in front of his eyes.

They were in what appeared to be a large, empty room. Every side was a blindingly white wall, and there were white tiles underneath.

Winnie clung to his arm. "What is this?"

T.T.'s voice echoed from ahead of them. "Keep coming, right up to here. It'll be easier in a moment."

Ahmad squinted as they moved through an archway. For a moment, the light was directly in his eyes and he couldn't see a thing.

And then, he gasped, stunned.

"What is this place?"

"What remains of Lailat," T.T. said hollowly. "The district of dreams."

Vijai Bhai stopped and stared, his face shattered like a broken mirror, his breath ragged and torn.

It was a sandy wasteland, dotted with blown-over tents and abandoned houses. Well, "houses" was maybe too nice of a word. They were more like sheds, formed with flyaway pieces of wood and tin. A low, mournful wind rolled over the terrain, brushing up against their cheeks like it was the first suggestion of warmth and company it had in a while.

Seeing what was all around them, Ahmad was sure it was.

"This is the district of dreams?" Winnie repeated. "It looks more like the type of place you'd see in a nightmare."

"It wasn't always this way," Vijay Bhai said softly behind her. He knelt down, letting the sand slide through his fingers. "There was a carousel, and a man who sold liquid moonlight. On some nights, there would be fireworks. On others, if you listened, you could hear the desert singing to you."

"So why get rid of it?" Winnie asked. "If it was such a wonderful place?"

"It was a wonderful place, but not in the Architect's eyes." Vijay Bhai shook his head. "The majority of the inhabitants were poor people. They didn't care to bow and scrape and beg him for more than what they had, and I think he wanted them to. He didn't like the fact that they managed to be so happy when they didn't depend on him."

"I'm surprised any of this is still here," T.T. called behind Ahmad as he waded through the sand toward one of the tents. As he drew closer, he could see gaudy stripes and tattered sheets of what must have been posters before. Was it one of those sideshow exhibitions those boys earlier had on their game? "The MasterMind unraveled most of this from the code quite early on, with the Architect's blessing."

Ahmad lifted one of the limp flaps of paper. On the back, an animated drawing of a bodybuilder scowled and shook his fist, but something about the movement was defeated: almost like he was going through the motions without any real anger behind it.

"It's odd to call it a blessing," Vijay Bhai said distantly. It didn't seem like he was speaking to any of them at all, staring out with clenched fists over the wasteland. "It seems more like a curse. All of this was so beautiful, and look at it now."

"It's terrible," Ahmad whispered. "This is terrible."

It hadn't sunk in until now, in spite of all the MasterMind's jeering and what they heard of the Architect's malice and temper tantrums. But now it did: They were dealing with people who could care less about other lives, whether they were computer-generated or not. If it didn't fit in with their plans, it wasn't worth valuing.

That could be this dark, dim corner of Paheli, or the wide, bustling world Ahmad knew: his beloved city, and everything that lived in it.

As though reading his thoughts, Winnie burst out, "This won't happen to New York City. We won't let it!"

"Brave words," an unfamiliar voice rasped from nearby. The words pelted against their ears like tossed pebbles, and they all lurched to attention.

"Who was that?" Ahmad gasped.

Vijay Bhai rested a hand at his side, as though he expected to find a sword or dagger hanging there. "Yes, who was that? Answer now."

"It's been a while, balloon man," the voice said.

A shadow unfolded from next to one of the collapsed tents.

It took Ahmad a moment to realize it wasn't a billowing fold of cloth, but a man: a small sad shade of a man, thin from his head to his shins. His face was drawn and pale, and his lips looked a bit too red, as if the wind had been smacking them like an open palm.

He looked like he had one foot in the grave. Or like he'd perhaps recently crawled out of it.

"Well, well, well," Vijay Bhai muttered, lowering his arms. "Mr. Titus Salt. What are you doing out here?"

"Titus Salt?" Winnie asked cautiously. "The guy you were looking for before?"

"He was the mind behind Paheli," Vijay Bhai said, not taking his eyes away from the approaching man. "Every gear went through his hands before it became part of the city."

"Still do, whether that upstart girl likes it or not," Titus Salt said. He spat over his shoulder toward a sand dune. Winnie winced.

"By that upstart, you mean . . . ," Ahmad started.

Titus waved a hand. "I have no time for whatever title she dreamed up for herself. She and the spoiled little master—sorry, our Architect, as if he ever knew what it meant to see this city built from the foundation up and know where everything was twisted and corked and set—may think they own this city, but I still am closest to its heart."

Ahmad realized the man was holding something. It was a small, golden gear. As he watched, Titus absently scratched its grooves, the way an old lady would groom her cat's ears. The gear actually seemed to shift in his grasp, like it was enjoying it.

It was creepy.

"The city doesn't seem to run on your gears anymore," Vijay Bhai said. "So why are you still lingering here?"

"She tried once to get me out of the code," Titus said, walking heavily toward an overturned barrel and sitting down on it. "She failed. As much as that boy can be a milksop, he knows what I mean in this city. My name, like that woman Nasirah's, is an important part of the game. It'll turn up at some point, and because of that, I've stayed rooted in here."

He looked around himself with disgust.

"What a shoddy job. It's taken days just to undo whatever she plucked out. Probably when she realizes I've restored it to this point, she'll just come in and wreck it all over again. But I feel I've made my point."

"You . . . restored this?" Ahmad asked tentatively. He didn't see anything that looked like it had been cleaned up, much less brought back to the old glory that Vijay Bhai seemed to seek in every dusty corner and destroyed stall.

Titus Salt gave him a withering stare. "Rome wasn't built in a day."

"I still don't understand," Vijay Bhai broke in again. He waved a hand backward, as though indicating the Paheli they had left behind. "I don't understand how any of that works out there. But I do understand that the world I knew, that I grew up in, has been demolished. There's not a familiar face to be seen out there. So how are you—"

Titus Salt reached out and grabbed his wrist, fast as a snake striking in a nature documentary. Winnie shrieked.

"What are you doing?"

Titus Salt didn't pay her any attention. His gaze was fixed on Vijay Bhai.

"There are loyalties in Paheli, boy," he whispered. "You know as well as I do. When you're loyal, it does not go unnoticed. When you do your part in the game, you are more than a mere pawn. You are a cog in the gear. You keep it rolling. And those who need that gear to roll along won't forget that you deserve the oil as much as that gear."

Ahmad stared at him, confused. What did all of that mean? Was he talking about the Architect?

Vijay Bhai, though, had gone absolutely pale.

Titus Salt gave a terrible grin up into his face.

"It is not the Architect's world alone," he rasped. "Or have you forgotten who brought you here?"

Swiftly, faster than Ahmad's eyes could track, Vijay Bhai snatched back his wrist.

"You're playing a dangerous game, Titus Salt," he whispered, and Ahmad had never heard his uncle so angry. "I hope you realize that."

Titus Salt was still giving that horrible, horrible smile. "Aren't we all, young balloon man?" He cackled. "Aren't we all?"

Without another word, Vijay Bhai turned on his heel and started walking back in the direction they came from.

"Wait, is that it?" Winnie called after him. "But what about your balloons?"

T.T., who had been entirely silent, blinked rapidly.

"T.T.?" Ahmad asked anxiously. "What did all of that mean?"

"I'm not quite sure," the mouse squeaked softly. "But we need to move on now. This place makes me nervous when it's properly lit."

Ahmad turned to follow him as he scampered away but glanced one more time at Titus Salt. The man was crooning at the gear in his arms as though it was a baby, tramping over the sand toward one of the tents.

A shudder ran down Ahmad's spine, and he rushed to catch up with his friends.

"Vijay Bhai, what was that about?" he asked anxiously once they were back out on the main avenue. "What did he mean about the gears and the oil and . . ."

Vijay Bhai tapped Ahmad's head with his knuckles.

"Just an old man's ravings, kiddo," Vijay Bhai said with a grin. "Don't worry about it. I forgot how unhelpful that old creep could be."

But his smile looked strained.

In the dark, once they got back to the car, they fumbled in the glove box to find rather lukewarm rotis and perfectly charred kabobs. A gift from Madame Nasirah, no doubt. They pinched off the

bread half-heartedly and shared a skewer before nest-
ling together.

They didn't intend to sleep.

The Minaret would surely sound at some point.

But it didn't.

Restless and fearful, they stayed awake, waiting for it.

CHAPTER THIRTEEN

THE HISS OF THE Minaret slid down Ahmad's ear canal like a droplet of water. He awoke, trying to shake it out. He accidentally thwacked Winnie with an errant arm as he wiggled. She shot up, a groan on her lips.

"Ouch! Ahmad!"

"Sorry! But didn't you hear that?"

Ahmad blinked, feeling disoriented. The last thing he remembered, he had been trying to clear his mind from Vijay Bhai and Titus Salt's confusing conversation by distinguishing the programmed stars from what might have been layers of the real world—his world. It was unsettling to him how readily he was forgetting the actual sky. Not that there were many stars visible at all from Manhattan, where the city lights outshone them.

He remembered the blanket, and T.T.'s whistling snores, and staring until his eyes ached toward the distant Minaret, willing it to blaze with cold green flames. But now, there was dry earth under his hands.

Also, it was oppressively warm.

He sat up straight. Winnie did too, her eyes wide. They were in the middle of a jungle, bristling with garishly green foliage and tangled undergrowth.

The branches of a tall banyan swayed in the breeze, the pixel surfaces shifting with shadows in a way that made them seem real. There were bizarre trees nearby too, trees with trunks that glittered, as though they were injected with the genes of some deep-sea jellyfish, and had leaves shifting through every color imaginable.

"Great. Just great," Ahmad muttered, trying to smooth down his sleep-mussed hair.

Winnie's eyes were wide. "How did this happen? We were in the city!"

"I guess the Architect didn't want to wait for us to get here on our own time."

Apparently, they had slept right through the Minaret's call. The countdown clock was already sliding backward through livid red numbers above their head.

"What? That is so unfair!" Winnie finally seemed to be awake. "Wait, where is T.T.? And your uncle?"

They were nowhere to be found.

And there was nothing left of the previous level. The game had shifted its world completely, folding the outlines of the dock into a path through the dense underbrush. Only the boat remained, as out of place as shorts in a snowstorm.

But at the end of the path, something stood, flickering in the first rays of daylight. A person, watching and waiting.

Not the MasterMind, or even T.T. It was a boy with high arched brows, an imperious smirk, and dark-circled eyes.

The Architect himself.

"You!" Ahmad gasped.

"Well, I'm pleased to see that you've made it this far," the Architect said.

"In spite of all your little games and tricks," Ahmad

responded sharply. "Maybe you're losing your touch!"

The Architect puffed out his chest. "If anything, I'm stronger. I was weaker before, easily cowed and devastated by the game's undoing. But it's a new day, and you'd better prepare with everything you have. I'm not one to throw down the dice lightly, and every turn of this world will bring a twist of fate to light."

There was a dramatic pause.

"Oh, great," Winnie said, rubbing sleep from her eyes. "Wait, what happened?"

When Ahmad reached out and tapped the silent Architect on the shoulder, his fingers slipping right through the apparition, he shuddered back to life.

"Well, I'm pleased to see . . ."

"He's a hologram," Ahmad said grimly. "Apparently, he couldn't be bothered to come and greet us himself."

"In a way," T.T. said from behind them, and they both jumped. He had a tendency to appear out of nowhere, quiet as a mouse. "This is one of his new Shades—stop touching it, Ahmad!"

Winnie clutched Ahmad's shoulder. "Yes, don't bother with it. He's trying to scare us. I see a path. I think that is where we are supposed to go next."

"Ahem. Yes. I shall guard the boat in the meantime," T.T. said, stroking his whiskers, perhaps enticed by the lure of more chenna murki.

Ahmad and Winnie eyed him, and he recoiled defensively. "Listen! I may be fierce, but inside my heart, I am still little. I'm just a mouse in a big, very hungry world. You're human. You'll be fine."

"And what about Vijay Bhai?" Ahmad asked anxiously. "Do you know where he went?"

T.T. tittered nervously. "Ah, yes, well . . . he said he had a new idea about where to locate his balloons, and a few things he wanted to investigate. Don't wait for him. He is not officially a player, you see."

"I'm sure he'll be fine, Ahmad," Winnie said soothingly. "Like T.T. said, he's not a player so that means the game will probably save all its nasty tricks for us and leave him alone."

"Was that supposed to be comforting?" Ahmad asked with a raised eyebrow.

"It's all I've got right now, okay?"

Ahmad relented. "Okay. Fine. We'll see you later," he said to the giant, hungry mouse.

"Let's go, Ahmad."

They grabbed their knapsacks, clasped hands, nodded at each other, and started to wade through the underbrush.

The next challenge awaited.

CHAPTER FOURTEEN

ALABYRINTH BLOOMED FROM THE very ground as they gingerly tiptoed through the jungle. Shrubs brandished themselves out, sprouting heads of green hair. Before they could bloom, though, they were snipped neatly into natural fences by unseen hands.

Seeds clawed their way from the earth, became saplings and trees in the blink of an eye. Plants Ahmad could not identify hovered over trunks or spread out gaudy, highlighter-bright pastel petals toward the brooding sunrise.

Words glittered in the sky: TRIAL: ESCAPE THE MAZE!

A sprawling map began blinking in and out of

existence beneath the words. Ahmad could just make out a small red dot that proclaimed YOU ARE HERE and a swallowing mass of greenery around it before it died away, vanishing as quickly as it had appeared.

"I guess we just have to make our way out," he said.

"I was afraid you would say that. Ugh." Winnie picked her way through two bushes, shaking her head. "I'm the worst at stuff like this—like, cornfield maze field trips to Long Island, you know? I usually skip those."

Ahmad did too, but not because of the same troubles with navigation Winnie had.

"Well, at least we're together," Ahmad said. "Let's just make sure we stay together and don't get lost."

Winnie was about to respond. Then her gaze turned upward. Her breath rushed out. "Ahmad. Don't make any sudden moves."

Ahmad glanced up automatically, then recoiled. A hideous monkey dangled down before them, baring its teeth. Its fur was mold-green and mottled with patches of pink, raw skin. Every other inch of its body was branded with stitches.

"Whoa. It's a total Frankenstein," Ahmad said out of the corner of his mouth.

"Whatever it is, I don't like the looks of it!" Winnie whisper-shouted.

It hissed. Ahmad tossed his knapsack at it.

"Stay back!" he yelled.

That turned out to be a mistake. The creature's eyes narrowed in on the satchel, and it snagged the handle.

"Hey!" Winnie hollered. "Let go!"

It became a tug-of-war.

"Big mistake, big mistake, big mistake," Ahmad chanted as the thing's grasp on the bag became stronger. "Winnie! My fingers are slipping!"

Winnie backed up, looking around her desperately.

"Okay, okay, um . . . Hey! Let go!"

From nowhere, a disembodied hand grasped her wrist, sending her shrieking. She managed to shake it off, backing away, while Ahmad won the bag back from the monkey, which darted up into the tree. Winnie tried to follow but made it only one branch upward before she gasped, losing her grip and falling out.

"Winnie, are you okay?" he asked.

Winnie only clapped the dirt off her pants while shaking her head.

"Nope. Nope, nope, nope, nope, nope, nope."

"What happened?" Ahmad demanded.

Winnie gestured with her head without looking up. "There's a . . . ugh, I can't say it."

"What?"

Ahmad followed her gaze. Staring back at him, with nearly human annoyance, was a bird of paradise, its outlandishly long tail feathering back and forth just beyond the branch. He groaned.

"Oh, come on, Winnie. I thought it was a wild tiger or maybe a dragon waiting to roast us for breakfast."

"Come on yourself," Winnie snapped back. "I guess you haven't had a proper encounter with a rat with wings."

Ahmad's brow furrowed. She sighed heavily. "Pigeons, Ahmad! Keep up!" She tapped each of her points onto a tip of her finger.

"They are filthy. They probably carry disease. They eat whatever they can get." She looked properly annoyed—and disgusted. "Humans included."

"I always thought they were kind of cute," Ahmad reasoned. "And they know how to cross the street, which some adults can't even do."

Winnie stared at him. "They are literally called

flying rats, Ahmad. Do you think rats are cute when they know how to use the crosswalk?"

Ahmad bit his tongue and shook his head again. "Well, at least we shook off that monkey. I think I can take on a bird if it decides to swoop at us. This isn't even a pigeon. Let's keep going."

Winnie stomped after him as he continued on, but not before muttering, "So they can get rid of the entire dream district, but they have to keep *birds* in the code? I hate this place."

The bird wasn't the half of it. They sidestepped pockets of quicksand and shouldered through bushes that seemed to grab at them from every angle.

"I am never going to complain about the Bronx Zoo again," Winnie wheezed, pausing to run her fingers through the twigs tangled in her curls. "How far have we even gotten?"

Ahmad stared around him at the trees. "I really can't tell. I hope we're not going in circles. Wait, Winnie!"

He reached out and snagged her collar, dragging her behind the nearest tree trunk.

"What is it?" Winnie hissed wildly. "What's going on now?"

Ahmad pressed a finger to his lips and gestured toward the path. They watched as a lumbering figure slouched past. It could have been human, almost, if it wasn't for the creepy twist to its head—as though it were sitting on a broken neck—and the shuffling of its footsteps.

"Ghouls," Ahmad whispered. A vague memory from one of his childhood nightmares flashed through his mind: a hideously leering face and rotting toes floating in front of his eyes, before he was buried under a pile of moldy bones and dangerously sharp jewels. "Better watch out for those, too."

Winnie rolled her eyes. "If they bother us, I'll make sure they're sorry they didn't just rest in peace."

Ahmad had to be impressed at the fact that she was not creeped out by ghouls but had a hard time with birds.

No one was perfect, but it comforted him to know that Winnie had her struggles.

They stopped to rest against a tree. Ahmad leaned into the satchel to get the water bottle.

"Oh no! Ahmad!"

Before Ahmad could react, a wiry, stitch-scarred hand had snatched up the satchel.

"Not again!" Ahmad groaned.

Winnie took off in hot pursuit and managed to grab the strap, along with the monkey's tail. The monkey squealed, struggling and trying to scratch her while Ahmad gingerly tried to grab the water bottle on the other side.

"It's dropped the satchel, but it has the puzzle piece! Get a good grasp on it!" Winnie gasped around a mouthful of fur.

"I'm . . . I'm trying!" Ahmad's fingers scraped against the puzzle piece—once, twice. Finally, triumphantly, he grasped its neck and gave a good pull. It popped out of the jittering creature's fingers and into his hands. He rushed to shove it back into the satchel.

The monkey gave one final swipe at Winnie's hands and ran for cover. Ahmad rushed to her side. "Are you okay?"

Winnie looked at her clenched fingers for a moment, loosening them slightly to see what was inside. When she looked back up, her eyes were shining.

"Oh, I'm better than all right. Take a look at this!"

There, between her hands, was an elaborately carved puzzle piece. Ahmad furrowed his brow, confused. Hadn't he just put it away?

It hit him.

"Wait . . . so this is—"

Winnie nodded, her eyes shining. "It's the next one! See?"

Rather than the monkey's head, this piece featured its curved plume of a tail. Winnie slipped it in the satchel alongside the other piece they retrieved from the ground.

"Let's get out first. After that, we can figure out what we have to do to get the last piece," Ahmad decided. Grasping the satchel as tightly as he could, with an uneasy eye on the trees, he took Winnie's hand and led her out of the grasp of the trees.

CHAPTER FIFTEEN

GETTING OUT OF THE forest was more complicated than they thought.

"Ugh! Just . . . stop!" Winnie shrieked as she batted her hands at a snake slithering up her leg. It flickered its pink tongue at her, eyes intent on the knapsack at her side. "Ahmad!"

"I'm trying!" Ahmad panted, trying to steady his grasp on the slippery leather of the snake's tail. Every animal in this jungle seemed to be a pickpocket. Ahmad struggled to loosen the serpent's death grip on Winnie, but it took a strategic stomp on its wiggly tail to send it scrambling back into the thicket.

If it wasn't some wild creature, there were the ghouls. Ahmad couldn't decide if they would be better if they actually tried to cause harm. Instead, they lurked out of view until they figured out the right moment to pop up, right in your face, and scare you silly.

"They are not going to get me this time," Winnie said fiercely after the third ghoul had scampered off, leaving them both shaking at the knees. "You hear me? You are not going to—ahhh!"

That wasn't even the last time.

"Think positive," Ahmad said to himself firmly. "Think fun. This is a game, right? Games are supposed to be fun!"

"This game didn't get the message," Winnie groaned.

He couldn't argue with her. It was as though Paheli was determined to ruin things that should have been, in theory, quite entertaining. Being chased by ghouls was perfect in a haunted house. Seeking out puzzle pieces wasn't a bad way to spend an afternoon.

Putting that together with angry birds and zombie monkeys in the middle of the hottest, most tangled jungle ever known to man?

Well, there was really no way to put a good spin on *that* situation.

A wrong turn here, a twisted pathway there, and

more than a few monkey fistfights later, Ahmad and Winnie broke free of the forest's grasp.

Winnie let out a sigh of relief at the sight of the entrance to the souk. "Oh good. We're back to civilization," Winnie said.

"Or as close as we can get right now, anyways," Ahmad pointed out. He took the puzzle piece from Winnie and turned it in his hand thoughtfully. "I guess our next step is figuring out what we do with these once we have them. That monkey was pretty intent on swiping these."

"That can be *your* next step. If I remember correctly from your map, Madame Nasirah is right down this corner. And I'm starving."

"Really? After all the fuss over the tea last time?" Ahmad asked.

Winnie's face pinked. "It was actually good tea," she muttered. "And don't you want to find out what happened to your uncle?"

Ahmad felt a guilty twinge. With all the battling they'd done to get through their challenge, he had forgotten about Vijay. Winnie was right. Madame Nasirah's shop was the most likely place for him to wind up, particularly in a world that had changed since the last time he was part of it.

"All right, then," he agreed. "Let's go."

It turned out to be farther than they assumed. They jostled their way through the crowd of holograms, watching shops appear, flicker, and disappear, and crowds of holograms gather and wander and bump right into them. It seemed like the people of Paheli had nothing else to do besides perpetually shop, all day, every day.

Hours had passed, or so it felt, by the time the kids staggered through the entrance of Madame Nasirah's shop. They dusted themselves off and collapsed onto the cushions, letting their heads loll back as they took a moment to breathe.

Madame Nasirah bustled out of the back entrance.

Ahmad smiled, readying the greeting on his lips—and there, the words froze. Because the woman was indeed holding her familiar teapot, but the look on her face bore not a drop of recognition.

"Oh my!" she crooned. "New players! Why, it must be an age since I've seen some young faces in the game. Welcome, welcome! Just give me a moment and we'll have some hot tea—chai for you, and lemon for you—and get down to brass tacks."

"Madame Nasirah—" Ahmad said.

"Why, why yes! Hmm, I suppose with all these new gadgets and doodads, they probably have to add in an instruction manual or two to keep the players' heads on straight. I am indeed Madame Nasirah, your Gamekeeper, and I am here to let you know how—"

The words and the woman both froze. It took Ahmad a moment to realize that Winnie was standing there, grasping Madame Nasirah's wrist. He hadn't even noticed her slinking forward, eyes narrowed and jaw set.

"That's enough, Madame Nasirah," Winnie said, holding the woman's gaze steadily. "Cut the act. It doesn't suit you."

"I have no idea what—"

Winnie held on, it seemed a little more tightly, and continued to stare in a way that would have had Ahmad shifting uncomfortably in his own skin.

"Yes. You do. Believe it or not, I know a lot about people pretending. I know about them pretending things are okay when things really aren't. I know about them acting like they can't see you when they can. I know that really well."

Something else occurred to Ahmad. "Wait! You remembered our tea orders, too! And you haven't poured from the pot yet!"

"I don't know—" Madame Nasirah started indignantly, but Winnie shook her wrist.

"Don't lie to us. You know who we are."

After a long, charged moment, Madame Nasirah looked away and shook her head wryly. The pot bobbed up and down in her hands. A grim smile tugged at her lips.

"Yes. You're right. I do. I'm sorry, my dear. There are certain roles I must take on in this world, as do you. But you will continue to find that out for yourself."

"Why?" Ahmad persisted. Winnie kept her hard gaze fixed on Madame Nasirah, seemingly more angry than anything else. But Ahmad felt shaken. Having Madame Nasirah not recognize them after a whole sea of people knocking into them with their elbows and shopping bags was more than scary.

It felt as though they had lost the entire game, and it was the first day of the rest of their life in Paheli. An endless cycle of days destined to repeat themselves.

Madame Nasirah sighed.

"There is never a moment where you are not watched here. Every weakness revealed is a chink in your armor to cast a spear through. Every wrong step will lead into an uneven cobblestone being placed in that very spot so you can trip again. And remember, there's someone who enjoys your pain enough to want to see it replayed."

"That is terrible," Ahmad whispered. "There's no moment to entirely be yourself."

"If I'll be honest with you, Ahmad . . ." Madame Nasirah paused. She suddenly looked very tired and very old. "I am no longer sure when I was last myself. But I try. All of Paheli tries, from day to day."

Ahmad nodded and put a hand on the old woman's arm.

They had to win. For her and everyone else who lived in this city.

"Even the Gamekeeper gets treated that way?" Winnie finally spoke up.

Madame Nasirah looked at her and nodded. "There's no one here who isn't a pawn for the Architect."

They sat in silence for a moment until Madame Nasirah cleared her throat and tried to muster up a smile.

"Well then, enough about that. You're just in time for fresh falafel sandwiches and some of my home-made hummus. Eat up and please make the shop your home for the night."

"We appreciate that," Ahmad said. Winnie was oddly silent.

"Good, then." Madame Nasirah tugged aside the curtains and looked out at the beautiful neon city and the circling sand winds, her brow furrowing. "Because I have a feeling you'll need a good rest to face whatever comes for you in the morning."

Before she could leave, a thought occurred to Ahmad.

"Wait, Madame Nasirah!"

The woman turned and looked at him expectantly.

"Did you happen to see my—ow, ow, ow!"

Winnie smiled pleasantly as her heel pressed firmly into Ahmad's toes.

"He was wondering if he left his lantern here, but I have it right here in my knapsack. You should have checked both bags, silly!"

Ahmad grunted between clenched teeth.

Madame Nasirah chuckled and shook her head. "You kids."

As she moved into the kitchen, Ahmad grabbed Winnie's shoulder and shoved her away.

"Hey, what was that for?"

"Sorry," Winnie said with a wince. "Was I too hard?"

"Of course you were—but whatever. What was going on there? Why didn't you let me ask about Vijay Bhai?"

"Shh, keep it down!"

Winnie gazed anxiously toward the kitchen door, where they could see Madame Nasirah humming to herself as she arranged their meal on one of her wide silver trays. Ahmad's stomach growled as he caught sight of a heaping platter of pita, topped with generously spiced chicken breasts.

"I don't know. Not yet. We need to stay alert. There's just something about this that doesn't feel right."

"What do you mean by 'this'?" Ahmad asked.

Winnie narrowed her eyes. "I just don't know. Her little amnesia act, something about the way she looked at us to see whether or not we believed it. It just feels strange to me, Ahmad. Can't you trust me on this one?"

She turned to him, her eyes pleading.

"We made a promise, remember?"

Ahmad huffed out a breath. He remembered, just as Winnie remembered how well he could draw in class and always seemed to think the best of him in spite of his overly quick tongue and how easily he could be distracted.

"Okay. I'll follow your lead. But Vijay Bhai—"

"If he turns up, we explain it to her then," Winnie rushed out. "But isn't it weird to you? She's supposed to know when new people enter the game, but she never mentioned him at all to you."

"He's not a player, though."

Winnie waved it off impatiently.

"There's no rest for us here, not when the rules keep changing," Winnie said with a sigh. "We've got to stay alert so we can figure out what's next. Keep your eyes and your ears peeled. Vijay Bhai will turn up, but in the meantime, we need to rest up for tomorrow."

Ahmad was about to respond, but Winnie shook her head, silencing him as Madame Nasirah brought in the tray, humming to herself. "Your dinner, my dears. Eat up. You'll need all your strength tomorrow."

CHAPTER SIXTEEN

AHMAD AWOKE TO A scrabbling in the dark.

For a moment, a brief, irrational, blissfully warm moment, he thought it was mice. Of course. That's what he got for sneaking snacks into bed during his late-night gaming sessions. Ma would be so mad at him.

I warned you about this! she would say.

After all, mice would be mice. The lure of food was absolutely irresistible to them, even in the wilds of the Upper East Side, where death traps lurked, well, everywhere.

Death traps.

Ahmad's eyes snapped open.

He wasn't in the Upper East Side. The mice—the

kind guardians of their journey thus far—were a furry, softly snoring heap in the far corner of the room.

They had snuck in late, feasting on cake rusk and anxiously sharing their fears about the eerie stillness of the city while Ahmad and Winnie counted and recounted their equipment, tucking away their precious puzzle pieces.

"Not a soul to be seen in the souk!" one had squeaked.

Another chimed in, "And all the floating footbridges are empty!"

"Is that what those are?" Ahmad had broken in with interest, remembering the delicate structures he'd seen during their walking tour of Paheli, bobbing toward a group of pedestrians waiting impatiently on the roof of a skyscraper.

Winnie had nudged him in the ribs with her elbow. "Ouch! Winnie!"

"Focus, you nerd," she'd muttered without looking up. "I lost count."

She didn't seem as focused on her task as she claimed to be, though, and Ahmad had wondered if she was maybe just as unnerved as he was, hearing about the deserted streets outside.

"But everyone can't be gone, right, T.T.?"

He'd turned to their intrepid mouse friend, who squeaked, cake rusk crumbs spilling down his sleek chin.

"What? Well—"

Ahmad had angled his chin toward Winnie and made wide eyes.

"Oh, yes, yes!" T.T. had chittered. "This has happened before. At least, I think it has. And all was perfectly fine in the end, I think! Sure, there were craters and avalanches and more sandstorms than you could shake your tail at, but . . . well."

T.T. had definitely been no help.

But now, even Winnie dozed. Ahmad trained his eyes across the room, trying to make sense of the fuzzy shapes and sounds. Everything was quiet. Too quiet.

Madame Nasirah was nowhere to be seen. Perhaps she had curled up somewhere too, her shawls and layers forming a delicate chrysalis around her tired body.

No. It was just him, the artificial moonlight, the

cluster of tea-related artifacts on every spare shelf and windowsill and countertop—

The shadowy figure, standing over his satchel.

"Hey!" Ahmad snapped, pulling himself upright. The figure froze. Ahmad rushed forward, determined to snatch its arm, but in a mere blink, it was gone.

Ahmad blinked. Everything was soft and still. Winnie hadn't even stirred at his exclamation.

He rushed to the bag, yanking out the equipment and quietly taking stock. After a moment, he leaned back on his heels. Nothing was missing.

Nothing except for, of course . . .

He touched his pocket. The puzzle piece was there, a satisfyingly heavy lump of marble and jewel. He had taken the one with the elegantly curved monkey's tail, bordered with ruby shards.

Winnie had tucked the other, with the monkey's head and its polished gem eye, in her own pocket the previous night. Both of them locked eyes and nodded solemnly. Behind them, the mice watched and anxiously rubbed their paws together.

"The Architect is acting oddly," Winnie had said then. "We can't take any chances."

"Are you sure this is necessary?" Ahmad ventured. He trusted Winnie, of course, who never misplaced her pencils on a test day or ran out of Scotch tape when she needed it most. But he couldn't quite trust himself the same way.

"Ahmad," Winnie had said softly. "Remember what Madame Nasirah told me. We have two enemies out there—maybe more. We can't make ourselves enemies too."

Her eyes had drifted toward the kitchen, and, even now, it struck Ahmad as odd. After all, Winnie had seemed to like Madame Nasirah, enough to suggest in the first place that they double back to the shop.

But they were in this together, and he had agreed not to tell the Gamekeeper anything. Even the transferring of the puzzle pieces had been done while her back was turned.

"Ahmad?"

Ahmad whirled around, drawing his hand quickly away from the hidden treasure. Madame Nasirah herself stood in the doorway.

"Is everything all right? It's rather late to be up."

"I thought I heard something out there," Ahmad

half lied, feeling guilty for the shakiness of his breath. He could feel his palms itching, that familiar twitch of anxiety and restlessness in his fingers. He jumped back from the wall as it suddenly shook with a gust of wind and the telltale scritching of sand.

"At least that is a familiar remnant of the old Paheli, as I always knew it to be." Madame Nasirah reached past him, and he quickly moved back as she checked the shutters. "The sandstorms at all hours."

"It was like this every day?"

"Well, particularly at night. It tends to be a sign of the Architect's temper. The weather is especially bad when things aren't going his way."

Ahmad's brow furrowed. Winnie was right. Madame Nasirah had told them that to begin with. He felt unsettled but couldn't explain why. They did have two puzzle pieces, after all, so the Architect should be seething or cooking up something particularly terrible for them to face next.

But all he had done was send a measly rabid zombie-monkey or two after them, and then sulkily refuse to sound the Minaret. Ahmad couldn't quite unravel his reasoning.

Madame Nasirah stepped away from the window. Ahmad reached out to draw back the curtain.

"You won't be able to see anything," she warned. "The storms usually hit quite thick and hard at this hour."

Ahmad looked out anyway. He couldn't explain why. It felt like he had to witness what was out there.

The clouds of dust parted under his gaze.

Ahmad pressed himself against the glass, his eyes wide.

There was a small boy in the midst of the sand.

"Who is that?" he wondered aloud.

"What's wrong, Ahmad?" Madame Nasirah's hand landed on Ahmad's shoulder, trying to draw him away. But he clung to the window frame.

"No! There's someone out there!"

It was hard to make out the boy's face, but his body was hunched and huddled down against the storm. He seemed scared. Lost. Alone.

Trapped.

Ahmad's heart pounded. Was this a vision, a way of messing with him? If he kept staring, would the boy materialize into a small child with a cake-sticky mouth from a birthday party he, only moments ago, had been careening through? Would he have his father's ears and his mother's cheeks and tears streaking his face from crying for his big sister?

Was that dream . . . a real dream?

The sand died for just a moment.

Just a moment to realize that he was wrong.

It wasn't a version of him, a younger Ahmad.

It wasn't a memory, or a nightmare, or a trick.

It was the Architect.

He was smaller and thinner, but his clothing was well tailored, carefully stitched, and his face was still smugly round. His eyes, even through the storm, were locked on Ahmad's.

They continued to stare at each other as the storm picked up once again. The Architect—or at least, this younger rendition—seemed to mouth something. Ahmad squinted.

What?

But before he could make out the words, the boy threw up his wrists to shield his face from the swirls of sand that spun around him. He faded away with the winds of the dying storm.

"Ahmad? Ahmad, are you all right?"

Ahmad turned around and faced Madame Nasirah. Underneath her protective layers of gauze and gathers, her expression was inscrutable.

"Didn't you see—"

"See what?" She drew the curtains. "There are a great many things to be seen in the sand, and not many of them are true. Remember that, Ahmad. Most of this world, more than ever, is made up of smoke and glitter and dreams that will never come true."

Ahmad couldn't shake away the image of brown skin and dark hair vanishing into the whirling sand.

Was that an omen?

And if it was, what was it supposed to mean? A foretelling, or a cry for help? What type of game *was* this?

"Do you need tea?"

"No," Ahmad said quietly. "I'm going to try and get sleep. Thank you, Madame Nasirah."

But as he curled back up next to Winnie, the questions bubbling over in his mind were enough to keep him awake until the early hours of the morning.

CHAPTER SEVENTEEN

B Y THE TIME MORNING—WITH its hustle and bustle on every street corner—had started to settle into early afternoon, Ahmad and Winnie were getting antsy.

They had attempted to make the corner of the tea shop that faced the Minaret their base. Nothing too fancy, just a nest of sheets and pillows and their knapsacks neatly tucked into a corner, ready to be claimed at a moment's notice.

In spite of the previous night's storm, the sky was clear and calm. Madame Nasirah, at least, had returned to high spirits, happily pouring tea and fresh steamed milk delicately from one of her etched carafes, served alongside hot spinach pies. It was not a comfort to Ahmad.

"Five . . . six . . . seven . . . ," he mumbled to himself.

He anxiously fiddled with the satchel in his lap, taking inventory, making the hologram flare upward with its small blast of air that made Madame Nasirah jump and clutch her scarves.

Winnie, on the other hand, paced.

Back and forth and back and forth and back and forth.

It was on her fifth round through the tiny shop that Madame Nasirah put her foot down.

"Enough. If you need to stay busy, I'll give you a task."

Madame Nasirah reached into a drawer. Ahmad's eyes widened as she pulled out sheets of blank paper.

"You like drawing maps of Paheli, right? Try and fill these in while you walk through the city. Keep track of what's shifted during the night. It might be a clue as to what the Architect is planning."

"Oh man!" It felt like years since he had gotten to chart out his beloved city—the Paheli that lived in his mind, rather than this waking nightmare. Ahmad eagerly took the sheets and the proffered pen that went with them.

"I wonder if I still know where everything goes!"

Winnie, however, narrowed her eyes suspiciously.

"You want a map of the city? But you're the Gamekeeper! Shouldn't you know where everything is? Or if it shifts?"

Ahmad tugged on Winnie's arm, his ears burning. "Winnie!"

Madame Nasirah chuckled. "Gamekeeper in name alone, I'm afraid. The more you children move about this world, the more I've realized how much of it has transformed around me."

Ahmad and Winnie looked at each other. Ahmad tried to telepathically message Winnie with his brain.

Knock it off.

It felt silly, jumping out of their skin at every word the woman said. After all, she was the only person in this world who had thought to help them at all. Could they really not trust her?

"All right," Winnie decided. "We'll help while we wait for the Minaret to sound. But we're not going on foot."

Ahmad didn't like where this was going.

A few minutes later, he didn't like the speed they were going either.

"Winnie! Winnie, slow down!" he hollered, clutching his seat rest with both hands and squeezing his eyes shut.

They had reclaimed their flying rickshaw, and Winnie was enthralled with playing pilot once again. "Oh, come on," she scoffed. "Don't be such a baby. My dad goes faster when we are on the L.I.E."

Her foot pumped on the gas pedal as Ahmad peeked out from beneath his lashes. He squeezed his eyes shut, trying to focus on keeping his very delicious breakfast down. His stomach lurched. And Vijay Bhai hadn't turned up yet. There was no note, no awkward bumbling through the door, and no sign. It didn't make sense.

Winnie insisted that the Gamekeeper shouldn't know that his uncle was even in the game, but Ahmad was no longer sure. Shouldn't they tell the one adult in here who actually cared if they were alive or dead? Maybe she was too focused on them to notice that Vijay Bhai had entered the game with them.

Winnie took a hard left and Ahmad's head jerked against the glass. He blinked the stars out of his eyes.

"What happened?" he demanded.

Winnie turned and looked at him ruefully. "Traffic."

Sure enough, there was a long line of floating cars trailing off into the near distance. Ahmad groaned and sunk into his seat.

"Great. It figures."

"Never mind," Winnie said sunnily, her smile returning to her face. "We've already seen most of this main avenue by foot anyway. How about we try and find a shortcut instead?"

Ahmad sat up straight. "Wait, I don't think you should—Winnie!"

She was already steering out of the line, ignoring a few horns being blown in her direction—and man, it was weird that the sound was comforting to Ahmad—before sidling in between two buildings and cruising down an unfamiliar street.

For once, the car maintained a good speed, and Ahmad craned his head, looking down with interest. This street wasn't full of the familiar shops. He did see what looked to be a restaurant or two: not with fancy metal tables outside or sunlit balconies, but small lines of people waiting eagerly for packed bags and little containers.

"Fast food," he whispered to himself. It warmed him. Paheli still had some good city roots to it after all.

But something else caught his eye.

"Wait, Winnie. What's that?"

He pointed, and then regretted it, as the entire car slid to the side along with Winnie's eyes.

"The wheel! Keep hold of the wheel!"

"Okay, okay! Sheesh." Winnie peered over it owlishly. "It looks like some sort of alleyway. We can go through it if you want."

Ahmad could only nod. He was sure he'd seen a flash of bright neon blue, like the sparks that flew when you tried to plug a charger into a slightly dented and twisted wall socket. There was something down there.

Something different.

Winnie took the car down lower, and Ahmad gasped.

"Look at that!"

"Oh man," Winnie muttered. "What *is* it?"

She descended to street level, narrowing her eyes as the car hovered.

"Dad always drew the line at me being able to

parallel park, because he said he didn't want to be part of the news story: 'Twelve-Year-Old Steals Parents' Car and Goes on Joyride Through Side of Building.' But I don't see why . . . Ahmad!"

She sighed as Ahmad, not waiting for the car to properly stop, leaped out the passenger side.

"It's a doorway of some sort!" Ahmad called back over his shoulder giddily. There was a strange electricity sparking through him. It felt like when he spent hours wandering over terrain in a new video game, trying to find the next quest—and then, suddenly, his controller gave a little jiggle in his grasp or his character found a new path to go down, and the adventure continued.

"I think we've been down this alleyway before," Winnie said, walking up to him. She frowned at the colorful neon archway looming over their heads. "Funny, I feel like I would have remembered this."

"You don't because it *wasn't here before*," Ahmad hissed excitedly.

This was their next challenge. He could feel it.

CHAPTER EIGHTEEN

AHMAD STARED PAST THE flashing neon doorway. He couldn't see much in the shadowy passageway that it led into. It looked like a cross between one of the rides at Coney Island and maybe a Halloween haunted house.

His heart pounded.

"This wasn't here before," he insisted. "Not in my sketches at home, and not when we walked this way toward Madame Nasirah's shop."

Winnie's face was doubtful. "We did do a lot of walking, and everything here kind of looks the same after a while."

"This is Paheli, remember? And it's a game. You

said before: If it sticks out, it must mean something. Maybe this is the challenge!"

"I don't know, Ahmad."

There was a hiss in the sky, reminiscent of Fourth of July fireworks. Ahmad and Winnie started, gazing upward at the red holographic timer. It was slowly ticking backward from ten minutes. The countdown had begun.

"Is that good enough for you?" Ahmad asked. "Remember that jungle level? We weren't even awake when that one started."

Winnie peered down the dark corridor. When she looked back at Ahmad, her jaw was clenched and she nodded her head.

"I guess we don't have much choice now."

Ahmad bent down and rummaged through the knapsack. "I wish we had some form of light in here," he grumbled. "Oh, wait!"

His fingers closed on the handle of the lantern. It didn't look quite like a lantern as Ahmad had seen them before in hardware stores. It was shaped more like the bulbous abdomen of a firefly, oval, with glass that had the transparency and separated segments of an insect's wing. When he tapped tentatively against its side, it beamed to life, each segment giving off its own hue of bright yellow.

"Wow," Ahmad breathed. "It's like a handful of sunlight."

He raised it up over his head.

"Yikes!" Winnie covered her eyes. "Put that away from my face, please!"

"Oh. Uh. Sorry."

Ahmad lowered the lantern and hoisted the knapsack back on his shoulder.

"Okay. Let's see where this takes us."

They tentatively stepped through the door, inching their way down another alleyway.

"You know, as creepy as this is," Winnie said, her voice a near-whisper as her hand trailed along the nearest wall, "it's also beautiful."

"Yeah," Ahmad agreed softly. Under their feet, the cobblestones glimmered as though they contained veins of precious gems, pulsing with electric reds and deep purples. It was some sort of futuristic version of the Yellow Brick Road.

There was an odd, static hum in the air too.

But what did it all mean, and where was it going?

"Are we sure this is not just a glitch?" Winnie asked anxiously. "Doesn't this remind you a bit of Lailat?"

"There was nothing left of Lailat to compare it to," Ahmad snarked back, but without much heat to his voice. For the first time since this whole game had started, the darkness felt reassuring rather than suffocating. It was as though they were venturing deeper into a cave, and sooner or later, they would stumble into the lit grotto where they would find a hidden jewel of a lake, or a special treasure, and everything would make sense.

There was a sudden shift in the shadows in front of him, and Ahmad gasped.

"What was that?"

"What?" Winnie asked wildly. "What did you see?"

Ahmad panted, his heart pounding. "I guess it was one of those . . . shadow things again."

"Does anything seem to be changed?"

The kids peered anxiously into the dark. The last times the shadows had appeared, buildings had shifted from sleek paneled sides to old carved stone, and sellers' awnings billowed out from slick nylon into threadbare silks. Now, though, Ahmad couldn't tell if anything had actually changed.

It made him even more nervous.

What were those things? More ghouls?

The wall nearest to them crackled and popped like rice cereal, and Winnie inched closer to him nervously. "I don't trust it. It has to be a glitch. How long is this thing?"

Ahmad was about to reply, but he stopped short.

"Oh. Oh, wow."

They had indeed found their way to a cavern, and it was ablaze with light from one central source: a maze. It rose up as a multicolored cube, walls towering toward the dark Paheli sky, which still bore the silently scrolling timer numbers.

"It looks like it belongs at the Met," Winnie whispered, and stepped forward to lay a hand against one of its sides.

"Winnie, don't!" Ahmad interjected, but her palm was already flat against the obsidian-colored wall.

"This doesn't feel holographic," she called over her shoulder. "You know, the way the other stuff feels like Pop Rocks against your fingers if you try to touch it? This is pretty solid."

Ahmad inched forward and gingerly laid his fingers next to Winnie's. She was right. As a matter of fact, the wall felt like solid stone. It had the grooves and smoothed edges that came with age.

Just the feel of it sent a shiver down Ahmad's spine, the tingle telling him he knew this stone better than he'd thought. It felt strange, but familiar, the thrum of energy it released making the hair on his arms stand straight up. He backed off, and surreptitiously wiped his hand on his jeans.

"All right, so . . . we made it. And this is here for us. Which means, this is the challenge, right?"

Winnie hummed, still looking doubtful. "I mean, the forest was a maze. It feels a bit redundant. But then again, a maze is a type of puzzle. It seems a little easy to just send us off on our merry way to find the exit."

There was a low rumble in the distance, from the direction of the entrance.

"Whoa, what was that?" Ahmad gasped.

Winnie backed away from the maze entrance.

"Whatever it was, it doesn't sound good. At all."

They stood there, together, waiting and listening.

There was no other sound. Ahmad shook his head and straightened up.

"Okay, look. This definitely is here for a reason. We need to go in there."

He reached back into his knapsack, fishing until he grasped the shrunken handle of the sword Madame Nasirah had dropped in. He drew it out, and then paused as something occurred to him.

"Uh, Winnie?"

"What?"

"If I pull it out, it'll get larger. I need some backup."

Winnie rolled her eyes and reached out. "Okay, let's do it together. We promised, right? But if there's anything like a dinosaur in there—oof!"

The supersized sword clattered to the floor and Ahmad lifted it up.

"We've got protection. Come on, Winnie."

She pouted, then shuffled along behind him. "All right, all right. Fine."

The kids turned back toward the maze and tentatively stepped in. Just beyond the entrance, there was a wrought iron gate, the kind that looked like it belonged to a botanical garden or one of those old mansions you could find in Park Slope or farther down Fifth Avenue.

Hanging off an intimidating, black-painted spike was a wooden plaque.

Winnie read it aloud.

"What you seek shall set you free. Don't forget the lock as you hold the key."

"Lock, key. Got it." Ahmad's mind was all for what lay beyond the gate. Neon light glanced off his excited eyes. "Let's do this."

Together, the kids pushed open the gate.

CHAPTER NINETEEN

I T ONLY TOOK AHMAD two steps to realize that the terrain was different.

It had more slide and give to it than the confidently placed cobblestones and sleek pavement of the outer world. One more step forward, just to hear that telling crunch again, and Ahmad knew for sure.

"Sand," he said.

Winnie reached down and let a handful slip through her fingers.

"It is!" she agreed, and then turned to him with wide eyes. "That is really weird, isn't it? Isn't the MasterMind all about the thick wires and huge sound effects?"

"Maybe this is another tug-of-war area," Ahmad

reasoned, though his mind wasn't really concerned with this new development. They were now in the thick of the maze, and everything in his body felt that there was something important waiting here for them. Winnie's words fell over him like an unwelcome rain shower pattering against a window.

The maze's interior didn't really give anything away. Apart from the constant light show and the sand underfoot, it was just . . . a maze. There was no writing on the walls, but there were arrows: large and as luminous as etched hieroglyphics on the side of an Egyptian pyramid, pointing every which way. They definitely wouldn't be of help.

That persistent, low hum hung in the air too. Ahmad shook his head to clear it.

"What's the rule about mazes again?" Ahmad broke into Winnie's nervous pattering, raising the lantern to try and see down the nearest corridor. "We stay to the left, right?"

"I thought we discussed this back in that awful jungle challenge," Winnie grumbled. "I'm no good with mazes. Hey, speaking of that, it's weird. Why are we facing two mazes?"

"What's wrong with that?" Ahmad decided on left and reached out to make sure Winnie was following behind him.

"Doesn't the Architect like to mix things up? And the MasterMind seems to pride herself on not being predictable."

"That is unpredictable, isn't it? Another maze—unexpected. Look, Winnie, I'm trying to concentrate," Ahmad started, and then stopped as the floor shifted under his feet. "Did you feel that?"

"No, no backtracking. What were you about to say?" Winnie crossed her arms over her chest.

"Winnie, I'm serious . . . Whoa!"

A real tremor shifted through the ground this time, enough to nearly unbalance Ahmad. He lowered himself to the ground.

"Do you think this is some sort of death trap?" Winnie asked anxiously. "Is it too late to mention that I'm not good with tight spaces?"

Ahmad had been doing well with not . . . well, being Ahmad. Now, though, he frowned and began, "Winnie, if you don't—"

It took him a second to recognize that the rumbling

had started up again, and now it wasn't just under their feet. It was echoing down the corridors toward them.

Something was coming. And it was coming fast.

"Okay, gotta go, gotta go," Winnie chanted, dragging him forward by the arm. They ducked into the corner formed by a wall and a dead end, and plastered themselves to the wall. Seconds later, the entire world bucked around them as, right where they had been standing, a large metal ball rocketed past.

It was like the boulder scene from that old *Indiana Jones* movie. Except there was no way to outrun this thing.

"Wow," Ahmad gasped. "Where did that come from?"

Winnie panted beside him. "I have no clue, but I'm just glad we didn't spin away with it."

Ahmad couldn't respond because something else had drawn his attention. Now that the ball was rolling off in the distance, that hum had broken through above everything else. As a matter of fact, it wasn't really a hum anymore. There was a steady *plop, plop, plop*.

It was like a running faucet.

Or a broken dam.

Ahmad rushed back into the corridor and stopped. Where the ball had rolled, it had shifted the sand spread underneath, revealing shimmering blue tiles. He held his shoe experimentally over the nearest one before lowering it down. As it settled, slight ripples moved backward from the heel.

"It's some sort of artificial river," Winnie whispered in awe.

"Yeah, but why?"

There was a glimmer beneath Ahmad's toes. He gasped and reared back. Where his shoe had been, a beautiful golden koi swam forward. As the kids watched in awe, it leapt up—right out of the tile, hovering in midair and catching purple light off its scales—before it landed in the next tile and vanished.

"How did it do that?" Winnie asked, but Ahmad had focused on something else entirely.

"Did you see that mark on its back? It looked like a key. The key! That's what we need to get. Come on!"

"Ahmad! Hey, Ahmad, wait!"

But Ahmad was already bounding off in hot pursuit. He didn't get too far, though. One wrong step, and his foot had landed on one of the water tiles.

Well, it didn't land. It went right through it.

"Cold, cold, cold!" Ahmad yelped. He yanked his leg upward, eyeing it suspiciously. Transparent droplets beaded up against his jeans and vanished without leaving any dampness.

"That is freaky!" Winnie said, catching her breath beside him. "Either way, now we know for sure we can't walk on water. It's the unbroken tiles for us."

"Okay, fine, but we need to keep up with that fish," Ahmad insisted. After giving his leg one final shake, he raced forward again. Shaking her head, Winnie followed.

"So just how are we going to catch that thing?" Winnie called as they hopped from tile to tile, pausing every so often as the ground trembled beneath their feet. "I don't think using our hands will work."

Ahmad turned to look at her. "Maybe—" he started, and then added, "Oh no." The earth was practically shivering beneath them, and this time, there was nowhere to move to.

In the distance, the large metal sphere bore down on them.

"Oh my gosh!" Winnie shrieked. "What do we do?"

Before Ahmad could reply, the sphere ricocheted off one of the walls in its path. There was a slow creak, like a deadbolt lock sliding out of its socket, and then . . . all the walls shifted.

"What is happening?" Winnie gasped, as the world collapsed around them, locking them into place.

Ahmad's eyes lit up as one of the last walls shuddered to a stop.

"That's it! You know those cheap little maze games they put in holiday goodie bags? There's a game like that I like to play online, only if the marble touches a certain wall, the entire thing changes."

"Great. Just great," Winnie huffed. "And now there's a wall there."

There was nothing else for them to do but slap the walls, trying to find another spot that would shift it back. It didn't help that just beyond the new wall blocking their path, they could see a small pool formed by newly crushed tiles—and the fish they sought happily bouncing up and down in the middle of it.

"It's laughing at us," Ahmad said sourly.

Winnie slapped her palm hard on one of the walls

closest to her. It shifted, and she turned to Ahmad with wide eyes.

"It worked!"

Unfortunately, that wasn't the only sound that met the kids' ears. Ahmad turned to Winnie. There was a creaky roar growing ever closer.

"That huge marble thing is coming back. Hurry, hurry, hurry!"

"This is moving so slow!" Winnie glanced over her shoulder. "Wait, is the sound coming from behind us or in front of us?"

Ahmad tried to put some of his weight on the wall. It still slid slowly, just parting so they could see the glorious blue of the pond waiting for them.

"I can't tell, but we need to move fast."

"If it can just move a little . . ."

Winnie waited and then, as the wall slid back, squeezed through the small opening.

"I'm in!" she called. "You next!" She grasped for his hands.

"Don't wait for me," Ahmad insisted, waving his hand as he stuck his leg through. "Run for the fish! We don't know when the maze is going to—"

The kids' eyes met with dread as a sound rolled down the corridor toward them: a low, dull rumbling.

"Move, move, move!" Ahmad yelled.

Winnie sprinted for the pond while he sucked in his cheeks and tried to slip through. The wall was still shifting frustratingly slowly. There was just enough space, though, if he could only . . .

There was a heavy thud, and then the rumbling stopped.

"Oh no," Ahmad gasped as the wall he was leaning against started reversing. He tried to tug himself backward, but he was stuck. "Winnie! Help!"

Winnie turned around and her eyes widened. "Ahmad!"

She started toward him and then paused, looking around frantically. She ran to the nearest wall and slapped it urgently.

"No, don't do that!" Ahmad wheezed out as the wall pressed firmly into his chest. "Just come here and push me back out!"

"Wait a moment, if I can just find the right—"

Winnie's hand connected with another wall. The walls stopped moving.

But Ahmad was still stuck in between them.

"Oh no. Oh no. Oh no," Winnie chanted. Her eyes were wild as her hands fluttered over Ahmad's face. "Ahmad, are you okay? Speak to me!"

"I'm fine," Ahmad managed, and then wheezed. "Just . . . really tight. Like a belt. Don't worry."

He managed to raise a finger and point toward the pond. Winnie groaned with dismay.

"It sank!"

There was nothing there but the slightest glimmer of blue.

"Go over . . . and . . . step on the tiles," Ahmad gritted out. "Hurry."

"But you're stuck here." Winnie hesitated. "What if that ball comes back this way?"

Ahmad widened his eyes at her, and she scurried off. She started to dance in the middle of the lowered tiles like a kid splashing in the middle of puddles.

"Oomph! Oomph! Oomph! Do you see anything yet?"

Ahmad made a grunt and hoped she could tell it was a no. He tried to focus on his own situation. He needed to get out of this jam before that huge marble came back. And fast. He wiggled his left foot, still protruding out the opposing end of the wall, experimentally.

Was it his imagination or was there a shaky tile under his heel?

Winnie turned to look back at him.

"Everything okay?" she called.

Ahmad managed a weak thumbs-up. She turned back to her puddle jumping as he slowly, painfully slid back his heel—

And then the passage started to tremble again.

Winnie gasped, "Oh no." Her foot came down hard on the ground. There was an audible splash and, though Ahmad's eyes were blurry from squirming against solid rock, he thought he could see the reassuring shimmer of cool water.

And something else. A flash of starlike gold.

"Grab it!" Ahmad called hoarsely. "Grab it, please!"

Winnie ducked down and held out her hands, like she was trying to coax one of those hated pigeons in Central Park toward her. The fish leapt upward into the air, shining between the gaps in her fingers like a ray of the sun. And then—plop, back into the water it went.

She looked up at Ahmad despairingly. "I missed it!"

"Try . . . again." Ahmad kept inching his foot back. Yes, there was a groove in the floor! He could feel it for sure now. He craned his neck around and gasped. "Winnie! Hurry!"

The ball was barreling down toward him.

Winnie grunted, her tongue stuck between her teeth. "If I could just—"

The fish's slippery body slid through her grip once again.

Ahmad kicked out wildly, hoping that his heel would manage to connect in time.

He didn't want to die here, not like this.

And then, he felt something give under his heel.

The walls eased back, and he tumbled through, and kept sliding forward on the slippery tiles.

"Winnie!" he hollered. "Look out!"

At the same time, Winnie leapt to her feet, a golden glimmer caught between her cupped hands.

"Got it!" she crowed, only to be cut off with a gasp

as Ahmad collided right into her. They tumbled into the center of the crushed tiles, feeling artificial wet and cold seep into their pants, and hugged each other as they turned to see the marble bearing down on them.

And then, the next thing Ahmad knew, they were falling through the floor.

CHAPTER TWENTY

AHMAD AND WINNIE SCREAMED as they tumbled and tossed down a watery slide.

"Where are we going?" Winnie called out, somewhere near Ahmad's ear. They were tangled up together, the precious fish slapping its tail against Ahmad's stomach and not at all helping with his queasiness.

"I don't know!" Ahmad hollered back.

Moments later, though, they rolled out onto hard cobblestones. Ahmad glanced up, recognizing the flying car parked near them.

"We're back out," he murmured, awestruck.

"And we still have our prize!" Winnie, looking a little wild-eyed and windblown, still managed to grin as she reached for the fish. Moments later, though, her face fell. "Huh? What happened to it?"

There was nothing resting against Ahmad's shirt but a shimmering jewel. Ahmad reached for it and held it up to the light. It glistened, first blue and then red, catching the light from the neon doorway. No key. And no lock.

He was disappointed but couldn't take his eyes off of the stone in his palm. "It's beautiful," he said in a hushed voice. "Do you think this is part of the monkey's eye?"

"Wait, you think this is part of the puzzle?" Winnie looked troubled. "Why would they give us some little extra piece instead of another carving?"

"I'm sure it fits in there somewhere," Ahmad reasoned. He reached for his pocket, but Winnie reached out and grabbed his wrist.

"Not here!"

"Oh, right. Sorry," Ahmad said, embarrassed. "So what do we do now, then?"

"What else?" Winnie stood and held out a hand to help him up. "We go back to Madame Nasirah's shop and see if we can figure this out."

Moments later, Ahmad was holding on to his seat rest for dear life as Winnie gleefully steered the flying car through the pink sky of Paheli.

"Do you really have to step on it?" Ahmad groaned. His tummy hadn't quite recovered from their last mission. But Winnie gleefully stomped on the gas.

In spite of her questionable driving, it did feel freeing to be out in the open sky. The oppressive nostalgia fell away from Ahmad's shoulders as he stared down on the city, watching the sun glint off the buildings—and, beneath their imposed frames, the familiar glass panes of New York City skyscrapers and monuments.

"Home is there," he whispered. "Waiting for us."

Winnie nodded, her face grim. "It is. And it knows we are here, fighting for it, so we can't give up, not now."

Ahmad turned to her, able to ask the question that had been weighing on him since the previous night. "You still feel it? That something is really wrong?"

"Of course I do! It's too quiet. Madame Nasirah is so twitchy, too. It makes me nervous."

"It might not be her fault," Ahmad pointed out. "She doesn't seem to have much control in this world."

Winnie sighed, and the rickshaw picked up even

more speed. "Maybe. I don't know. This world has me on edge. I don't like it. It doesn't feel like you can trust anyone here."

"You can trust me," Ahmad said firmly. "And I can trust you. We have each other and that's what we need. We promised, remember?"

"Right."

For a moment, they smiled at each other. From behind them, there came a piercing wail.

"Oh no!" Ahmad moaned.

"Are you kidding me?" Winnie exclaimed.

Because there, in their rearview mirror, was a car that—in spite of its ability to hover and flashy side emblem—could only be one thing, and the voice that bellowed in the moment afterward confirmed their suspicions.

"THIS IS THE SAND POLICE FORCE OF PAHELI. YOU ARE INSTRUCTED TO TURN YOUR VEHICLE TO CRUISE AND FIND A SAFE PLACE TO LAND TO BE QUESTIONED BY THE OFFICERS FOR ILLEGAL VEHICLE USE."

Ahmad leaned his head out the window. "We're players! We're supposed to be here!"

The shadowy figures in the police car did not move. After a moment's pause, the voice repeated, "THIS IS THE SAND POLICE FORCE OF PAHELI—"

"Forget it." Winnie jammed her heel on the gas pedal and the car lurched forward. "This is another Architect trick, I know it. Maybe this is about that jewel we just got. We need to get out of here."

The police car buzzed behind them. Ahmad anxiously leaned out the window. "We're players!" he called toward the car, cupping his hands around his mouth. "We're supposed to be out here!"

"Give it a rest, Ahmad!" Winnie hollered behind him. "They don't seem to care!"

What happened next had him quickly tugging his head back into the car. Two great cannons sprouted from within the police's car hood and deliberately aimed at his window.

"Whoa! They are going to shoot at us! Step on it, Winnie!"

Winnie pumped the gas and yanked hard on the wheel. They careened to the side, just as a great ball of fire shot out past where they had been and slammed into the side of a flying billboard. It exploded, glitzy bulbs and bits of screen raining out over the city.

"Hold on!" Winnie gritted out.

They raced through the sky, angling between buildings. The police car continued to volley out shots behind them. Ahmad hissed through his teeth as one narrowly bounced off the hood of their car.

"Ahmad! I need you to tell me if we're going the right way!" Winnie called. "I can't do this and think about directions at the same time. We need to shake them somehow."

"Okay, but—"

They both froze as a second whine joined the first car behind them, and a smug voice announced, "FUGITIVES OF JUSTICE, YOU ARE EVADING FOUR OFFICERS OF THE LAW OF PAHELI. YOU ARE ADVISED TO REMOVE YOURSELF FROM YOUR VEHICLE BEFORE WE CONTINUE WITH DUE FORCE."

"Fugitives?" Ahmad squeaked. He glanced down at the shimmering jewel in his hand. So he was right. This must be what they were after. But how could they be thieves and fugitives if they were supposed to find it?

Either way, he couldn't just sit there and let them be fired at like this.

"Due force? They're already shooting at us! Worse than the cops in New York. Ahmad, what are you doing?" The last was said in her now familiar, panicked shriek. Ahmad was halfway out the window.

"Playing it their way," he yelled back. "Hey, you guys in the clown cars! Bet you can't do this! Winnie, head through there!"

Winnie followed his pointing finger and gasped. "The Minaret!" It had its own raised platform in between two narrowly set, leaning buildings. If they could scrape through one of those passages, they would be able to make it back to Madame Nasirah's shop without their troublesome shadows.

The police cars sped up behind them. "Predictable," Ahmad yelled. "They are part of this world. Of course they can't resist a good challenge."

He leaned out the door, jeering at them, as Winnie jetted toward the passage. Ten feet . . . five feet . . .

"Ahmad, now!"

One final blast jetted out from the police car, colliding with the base platform of the buildings. It crumpled, heavy marble and thick wire swatting one of the cars out of the air like a fly. The others staggered and stumbled to avoid the debris.

Ahmad yanked himself back in as Winnie jerked the car to the side.

"We did it!" Winnie whooped.

And not a moment too soon. They heard the telltale screech and slide of skidding wheels and shattering glass behind them.

Winnie yanked on the brake and they slid in front of the alleyway, panting.

"That . . . was . . . awesome," Winnie breathed.

Ahmad was too busy looking at the front of the tea shop. It was too dark. "Winnie, I think something's wrong. Come on, quick!"

Before they could reach the front door, though, a shadow fell over them. Winnie gasped and grabbed Ahmad's arm.

"It can't be night already, can it?" she whispered.

Ahmad swallowed hard and braced himself for that awful pressure.

But instead, a screen scrolled outward, blotting out part of the artificial sky. It was a small black square that seemed as though it was painted on. Ahmad and Winnie stared at it.

"What—" Ahmad started.

And then, a figure slowly emerged from the black. An unseen camera zoomed outward from her small smirk and leopard-print bucket hat, and then outward to her camouflage vest and high pink boots. By the time it had panned out for a full-body shot, she was stepping out of the screen and down a set of unfolding stairs.

"The MasterMind," Winnie hissed. "What is she doing here?"

Ahmad couldn't answer her. Together, they waited as the girl approached them.

What could possibly go wrong now?

CHAPTER TWENTY-ONE

WELL, YOU SEEM TO be having a good time," the MasterMind purred. "Out for a little joy ride?"

"It's not like we had anything else to do," Winnie spat back. "What was the big idea, not giving us a proper announcement for a challenge?"

"A challenge?" The MasterMind put on a look of surprise. On anyone else, it might have been believable. On her it would have been comical—if Ahmad and Winnie hadn't nearly died completing the challenge. They glared at her.

"Give it up," Ahmad growled. "We figured it out already. You wanted us to waste time. I don't know why you and the Architect don't think you can win this without dirty tricks, but we—"

He stopped short with a gasp as a snake dropped from the air, out of nowhere, and snapped its mouth at his nose before falling downward into nothingness.

"The only one wasting time right now," the MasterMind said with that fake sweet tone, "is you. Both yours and mine. There was no challenge to complete, Ahmad Mirza. I simply don't know what you're talking about."

Ahmad's and Winnie's gazes followed her finger up to the sky. Winnie gasped in dismay.

There was a new timer—a different timer from the one that had hovered over the marble maze they'd scrambled through—and it was at forty-five minutes. And counting.

"I had given you a full hour. But I've taken fifteen minutes away, since you insist on being so contentious about every little thing," the MasterMind continued. "In any case, it seems you guys need to pay more attention."

"But what about this?" Ahmad insisted, fumbling in his pocket. "This has to prove that . . ."

His fingers collided with the object he was looking

for, and he drew it out in triumph, only to be shocked. Wait, where was the jewel?

"What is that?" Winnie asked, confused.

There was another monkey carving in his grip. This one, though, looked different from the others. It was lighter, and cheaper, with an almost plastic sheen as they held it up to the light. And then, as the kids watched in horror, it started to crumble.

"No! No!" Ahmad tried to hold it together with his fingers. "What's happening?"

"Oh, so I guess you stumbled onto my little decoy," the MasterMind cooed. "Too bad, so sad. That's not what you needed to get out."

"You tricked us?" Winnie seethed. "You actually tricked us?"

The MasterMind shrugged coolly. "No one ever said this game would be fair. Funny. You were supposed to stumble onto that earlier on. I guess I overestimated your intelligence."

Winnie growled, but all Ahmad could do was topple to his knees, stunned.

It wasn't real. They had faced down death and

scrambled after that ridiculous fish just for it to not be real.

"What about the jewel, though?" he asked dazedly. "Where did that go?"

For once, the MasterMind looked utterly confused. "What are you talking about?"

Before Ahmad could answer her, though, Winnie broke in.

"That whole challenge was just a setup? I can't believe you! What kind of game is this?"

"Fuss all you want," the MasterMind said, "but you're just hurting yourself. Now there is a challenge, and you're not even close to starting it. I would focus on that instead of how I handle my game."

"It's not yours, though, is it?" Winnie snarled.

The MasterMind's face flickered with anger for a moment, but she only gave an elegant shrug. "We'll see about that. Ta-ta for now!"

She swept her hand down her body, magically erasing herself away as she went. Before her fingers could even glide over her ankles, the MasterMind was gone.

"I can't believe this," Ahmad whispered to himself. "I can't."

He felt sick to his stomach. This was his fault. Winnie had warned him that it was too good to be true, but he had been so confident. He thought he knew better. And now, look what they had gotten themselves into.

Winnie leaned over him, her face concerned.

"Ahmad, are you okay?" she asked. "Here, stand up. Let's go into the shop and tell Madame Nasirah what happened."

Before they could reach the front door, though, the mice tumbled out, chattering and trembling.

"Madame Nasirah is missing!" T.T. chittered. "She never returned from the marketplace."

"What?" Winnie gasped.

One of the mice whimpered, "This is not normal at all."

Winnie's face, beside him, was shocked. Madame Nasirah was the Gamekeeper. She was the only person who, besides their adversaries, could see and interact with them—and, more importantly than that, actually *cared*. "What are we supposed to do now?"

Ahmad doubled over, panting and trying to stop his spiral. His brain wouldn't stop whirring with worry. This was too much. He couldn't take it. He just wanted to sit down, shut up, give up. Let them win. What chance did they have anyway, especially when the other side wouldn't play fair at all.

And, behind them, after an entire day of waiting, they heard the telltale firecracker spark of the Minaret. For real this time. Hearts pounding, Ahmad and Winnie turned their heads up to the sky and read the words etched there.

FINAL TRIAL: BALANCE BOTH SIDES OF THE SCALE. BE SURE NOT TO GET DISTRACTED BY MONKEY BUSINESS!

CHAPTER TWENTY-TWO

WAIT, NOW?" AHMAD GASPED in despair as the fireworks faded away. "How are we supposed to do this now? We have to find Madame Nasirah. And—"

"Ahmad!" a strong voice called in the distance, and Ahmad whirled around, hoping to see the Gamekeeper draped in her shawls. But the face he saw was also a welcome one.

"It's your uncle!" Winnie gasped happily. "Where have you been?"

Vijay Bhai jogged up to them.

"Sorry," he huffed. "I meant to be here sooner, but goodness, the time I've had trying to find anything in this new city."

"Vijay Bhai," Ahmad blurted out. "Madame Nasirah is missing. And we just heard a new challenge being announced but we need to find her and I—"

Vijay Bhai grasped him by the shoulders. "Whoa. Ahmad, breathe."

Ahmad tried, but he couldn't seem to. To his embarrassment, tears prickled the corners of his eyes.

"We thought we had the right challenge and we wasted so much time." And nearly died, but he didn't tell Vijay Bhai that. "It was all my fault. I believed it was the right challenge and it was all my fault."

"Ahmad, listen." Vijay Bhai tipped up Ahmad's chin with his finger. "These are the games played in Paheli. If you were tricked, it is not your fault. It happens. A lot. But I need you to take a breath and listen to me."

Ahmad stared into his uncle's eyes and took a deep breath.

"Good." Vijay Bhai smiled at him, clasping Ahmad's shoulders with his hands. "Now listen. You are a Mirza. There is no one who knows how to play—and win—a game better than a Mirza. There is no one who can be trusted more by their friends than a Mirza. The MasterMind and the Architect can play with you all that you want, but the only one who can stop you from losing is you. Do you understand?" Ahmad nodded. "Don't lose your faith now."

He looked at Winnie, who was wide-eyed. "Do you know how to get to the Minaret?"

"Yes, sir!" she said quickly.

"Good. Go there and start the challenge. I'll search for Madame Nasirah."

"But I—" Ahmad started.

"Ahmad," Vijay Bhai said firmly. "You need to win this. You need to end this. For all of us."

All Ahmad could do was nod. Vijay Bhai gave him a final clap on the back, smiled at Winnie, and bolted off in the direction he came from. After a moment, the kids did as well, heading in the direction of the Minaret.

There was no more time to waste.

The mice troop were way ahead of them as the kids approached the Minaret, panting and grasping their sides. They scurried and flailed their short arms, seeming to point this way and that.

T.T. pushed through, utterly exasperated, and managed to squeak, "The regiment has . . . rather fallen apart, I'm afraid! That sound brings out the worst of rodent instinct in them—steady on, Matilda, you needn't shove!"

He pressed through and Winnie and Ahmad caught up to him, following closely as he led them down a paneled boardwalk above the lower quarters of the city. Ahmad doing his best not to peer through the rickety wood slats into the dark quarry of tunnels and dingy buildings that lay hundreds of feet below them, beckoning.

"The instructions said we were supposed to head for the Minaret!" Winnie protested, but T.T. shook his head and tapped his nose.

"Smells like trouble that way."

"Sand Police?" Ahmad asked with a sinking heart, and T.T. nodded. "They might have been responsible for the announcement. They hold a grudge like nothing else."

"But what does it mean if the police have commandeered the game announcements?" Ahmad asked. "Where is the Architect?"

T.T. only shook his head. "I have no idea what is going on at all."

He led them toward another of Paheli's mysterious wooden doorways, bearing an ominous emblem of a sandstorm that the kids couldn't help but take note of, because their feet were sinking into what was indeed sand.

"Yipes!" Winnie yelped, and Ahmad grasped her arm for balance when he slid too far to the side. "This must be a desert level. So much sand!"

Golden letters shimmered before them in the air.

FINAL TRIAL: DO THE MATH AND AVOID THE MONKEY BUSINESS! BALANCE OUT THE SCALES AND YOU WILL FIND WHAT YOU SEEK!

"Great," Winnie muttered. "Math. I knew that was going to come up sooner or later."

"But you enjoy math class," Ahmad pointed out.

"Exactly. The game has ruined most of my loves in some form or another: our flying car, my mom's tea. I guess I'm lucky it hasn't broken out the Zelda or *Star Wars*. Yet. Well, let's do this thing. Where do we start?"

There was a rumble beneath their feet.

"Whoa! What's that?" Ahmad clutched Winnie's arm. The two of them rocked back and forth, trying to maintain their balance while not getting swallowed whole by the erupting ground beneath them.

A bizarre structure rose from beneath the sand: square and bricked in, it resembled a fortress, complete with what appeared to be pixelated soldiers marching back and forth on its walls. The mice cowered and chittered behind them, not daring to move forward.

In the building's courtyard stood a scale of gold, each side being tugged upon and bounced against by the same horrible zombie-monkeys they had encountered during the jungle level. They yanked at the arms of the scale and tossed themselves on and off the platforms.

"Ugh, return of our furry not-so-friends," Winnie groaned.

Ahmad groaned too, but for a different reason. A scroll blinked and flickered in front of him. "I have a feeling things are about to get much worse."

He reached out and tapped it once. It unfurled, and Winnie leaned over his shoulder to read too.

Race the rising sand! Balance out the monkeys on the golden scale—an accurate weight shall bring forth peace and an ebbing of the wind!

"Well, that sounds easy," Winnie said sarcastically.

"At least they didn't tell us to form a cheerleader pyramid with them or anything."

Ahmad frowned. "There must be a trick to it. It sounds too easy."

He was ever so wrong. There was no way it could have been worse. Because they had to get ahold of the monkeys first, and they were hardly feeling cooperative, running this way and that and squealing—shrieking, really—with delight and amusement as the kids tried to chase and capture them.

"Maybe we should grab them by the tail," Winnie suggested, already out of breath.

Ahmad gingerly reached out behind one of the creatures. "Easy does it," he gritted out. "Don't turn around, don't turn around—"

Another of its watching comrades let out a high shriek of warning.

"Ow, ow, ow!"

Ahmad was left sucking at the scratches and attempted nips left on his fingers.

"Oooh," Winnie winced in sympathy. "Maybe . . . maybe we should try to get one of those guys to help us! It feels like they got put there for a reason."

Sure enough, there was a neat row of soldiers on the fortress walls, standing shoulder to shoulder, many decked out in turbans and beautifully embroidered tunics, holding glistening swords at their sides.

"Hey! Um, hello up there!" Ahmad and Winnie hollered together, jumping and waving their hands.

It didn't take long for them to realize that it wasn't going to work.

"They haven't blinked," Winnie grumbled, lowering her hands.

"They are non-playable characters," Ahmad said. "That's disappointing. Maybe we could have used their spears to corral the monkeys into place. No one likes a pointy tip."

"Ooh, I'll show the Architect," huffed Winnie, rolling up her sleeves. "I'm done with being Ms. Nice Girl. Come here, you monkeys!"

She seized one bodily and, apparently shocked by the affront, it froze. Winnie held it aloft, beaming from ear to ear as though the creature in her hands were a gold trophy for excellent participation, and not a seething, moth-eaten bag of scientifically tampered-with bones.

"See! It's all in the wrist!"

The monkey quickly recovered and tried to seize up her arm with an outraged chitter. Winnie shrieked.

"Go long, Winnie!" Ahmad hollered, pointing frantically at the other end of the scale. "Go long!"

Winnie gritted her teeth, dug in her heels, and tossed the monkey out of her arms. The creature flew through the air, shrieking as it went, and landed in the lap of the scale, looking rather dazed as it settled in place.

"All in the wrist," Winnie repeated triumphantly. They high-fived.

By the time they had wrestled a few creatures and were bathed in their own sweat (and a bit of blood), that initial wave of triumph had washed away. They'd fought and measured and added and subtracted, and now seven monkeys sat on each side of the scale. But it refused to balance properly, and the wind continued to lash at their faces and tug at their clothes like a petulant child, frustrated they were trying to ignore its lamentations.

Ahmad threw up his hands in exasperation, not caring that the monkey he had been wrestling took the opportunity to scamper away. "This is not working."

"There's probably a trick to it," Winnie huffed, brushing her damp hair out of her eyes. "But what are we supposed to do?"

Something occurred to Ahmad. This was a game where they had been warned from the beginning that the rules always changed. So why were they still standing here, expecting fairness?

Why not assume that they were being set up from the very beginning?

Without answering Winnie's inquiry, Ahmad strode to the fuller scale, staring at the wriggling creatures. The monkeys looked up and hissed malevolently, exposing dripping fangs—except one, one that curled on its side and stared out at the rising sand, as though it couldn't be bothered to play the part.

Or . . . like it was playing its part, the way it was told.

Ahmad gritted his teeth and reached into the pile, narrowly missing a few pounces at his hand from the other monkeys, who seemed suddenly frantic. He fished about for a moment before grasping the bored creature's tail, yanking it free from the pile.

"It was hiding itself!" Winnie gasped as he held it aloft.

"Exactly. It's an extra, set in here to throw us off no matter what we did." Ahmad roughly tossed it aside, ignoring its chitter of outrage.

The scales tipped slightly to one side before settling. They were both equally measured out, finally, a fine balance. The monkeys upon them had stilled, holding a sulky silence.

At long last, Ahmad knew, he'd figured out the trick to playing in Paheli. You had to beat the game with its own tricks.

CHAPTER TWENTY-THREE

AHMAD AND WINNIE CLASPED each other's hands and danced around, tossing their heads back to shriek their triumph at the sky. They had done it, they had done it, they had *done* it. It was another step—perhaps the final step!—toward survival, toward freedom and home.

"Now let's find your uncle," Winnie said happily, "and GO HOME."

"Wait," Ahmad said, gently drawing his hands out of Winnie's. "Is it just me, or is it really quiet?"

Winnie frowned. "It is. Where are those monkeys? And where is the puzzle piece we earned?"

"Right here, on both counts."

"Whoa!" Ahmad hollered, and drew back, Winnie

backing up with him. They were surrounded by the zombie-monkeys, hair bristling and backs arched. The leader of them—the one that Ahmad was sure he had roughly tossed aside, moments ago, pounced in front of them, teeth bared and paws outstretched.

And it was the monkey that had spoken.

It took a moment for Ahmad to realize what it held between its teeth.

"Hey! The puzzle piece! That's ours!"

The monkey backed away. "Not so fast. There's something else you seem to be missing."

Ahmad and Winnie glanced between each other. "Uh, excuse me, Mr. Monkey," Winnie snapped, "but we really don't have time for riddles."

"And who told you just that?" the monkey asked, a smug tone to its voice that grated on Ahmad's nerves.

"Madame Nasirah, of course. Heard of her? She's the . . ." Ahmad's voice trailed off. "The Gamekeeper. The Gamekeeper disappeared and we haven't found her yet!"

"When all the pieces aren't on the board, there is a reason for concern," the leader monkey responded. He brandished the puzzle piece, and Winnie leaned forward gingerly. When he made no sudden movements, she took the piece, subtly wiping it off on her jeans.

"Uh . . . thank you. For the piece. And the advice."

The monkey nodded. But Ahmad had a question of his own.

"Back there, you were ready to tear us apart. Why help us and hand the last piece we need over now?"

"Everyone has their role to play," the monkey said. "Some more willingly than others." He backed up, and the monkeys moved expectantly with him. As they left, he turned and looked over his shoulder at them one more time.

"Stay on your guard. You aren't in the clear. Not by a long shot."

And with that, they moved back into the rising sand. The platform and its bizarre architecture, with a single rumble, receded into the earth.

"Wow," Ahmad said with a whistle.

"So now what?" Winnie asked. "Apparently, we need to find Madame Nasirah, but where do we begin? Where could she be?"

"Why," a familiar voice said. "I'm right behind you, dear."

The two whirled around. Sure enough, there stood the Gamekeeper, in her familiar endless folds of cloth, looking entirely untouched by the gusting wind and reddish sand that flew around her.

"Madame Nasirah!" Ahmad called, relieved. "You're all right!"

"Where have you been?" Winnie asked eagerly.

"In a meeting with the Architect," she said, picking her way delicately toward them. Under her veil, her eyes were solemn. "I'm sorry to have concerned you with my absence. There have been some . . . complications."

"What do you mean?" Ahmad demanded. "We got the last puzzle piece."

Madame Nasirah pressed her lips in a tight line, but before she could say anything more, there was a low lightning crackle from the edges of the city. Ahmad and Winnie whirled around, watching in horror as the Minaret sent up its green flare.

"It can't be!" Ahmad gasped.

"But we just finished the last challenge!" Winnie protested.

But there, again, was the spark of flame from the

minaret, and the words streamed out over the sky.

ALL THREE PUZZLE PIECES HAVE BEEN CLAIMED. AN ADDITIONAL TRIAL HAS BEEN DEVISED BY THE ARCHITECT IN COMPENSATION FOR AN INFRACTION OF PAHELI LAWS. PROCEED TO THE PALACE OF DREAMS. THE PIECES HAVE BEEN WON. IT IS TIME TO ASSEMBLE THE PUZZLE.

"When did we break a law?" Winnie sputtered. "If he means that joy ride with his police force, they were shooting at us! And that fake challenge was all his partner's fault too!"

"Like he would listen to that," Ahmad grumbled.

When he turned to look at Winnie, though, her eyes were shining.

"This is it, Ahmad," she whispered. "I can feel it. I don't know what else is going on, but we've gotten under his skin. We're making him nervous. I mean, why else would he feel the need to make Madame Nasirah disappear, to mess his own ground rules. If there's anything we know from the past, a player making the Architect worried about his hold on Paheli is only ever a good thing. We're going to win this, and he knows it."

Ahmad wasn't so sure, but looking at his friend's

calm and confident expression gave him hope. He nodded. "Okay. We're going to show this guy who's boss. But where is this Palace of Dreams anyway?"

"I can show you the way," Madame Nasirah broke in, making both of them jump. They had forgotten she was there. "It is the home of the Architect within this world, but now that he no longer shares it with his mother, the Lady Amari, it has been mostly abandoned. I would think that MasterMind finds it an eyesore, as the Architect refuses to let it be properly joined with the rest of her tricks and devices within this new Paheli."

"What happened to Lady Amari?" Winnie asked.

Madame Nasirah lifted one shoulder in an elegant shrug. "The last we saw of her, she was aboard her beloved sand train, attempting to escape the wreckage of the previous game with her son. But when he reappeared, he was alone. Maybe she abandoned him."

"Harsh," Winnie muttered. "Meanness seems to run in the family."

Ahmad's brow furrowed. That didn't seem right. Could a mother really leave her son behind like that?

Winnie tugged at his arm. "Ahmad! We need to get going!"

"Right." Ahmad squared his shoulders and faced Madame Nasirah. "Let's go."

They rushed through the silent city. The puzzle pieces weighed heavily in Ahmad's satchel while the quiet of the city troubled his mind.

Apparently, the Architect couldn't even be bothered to bring the souk back to life as they moved through it. Every stall was dark and still. Birdcages swung quiet and empty under white sheets.

Even if the people weren't real, even if they were only non-playable characters that could be turned on and off at will, it made him feel guilty.

And worried.

Winnie seemed to share his apprehension. "He must be real mad now," she muttered softly.

"Here we are," Madame Nasirah said briskly, pointing upward. Ahmad and Winnie squinted at the sky. She had led them to the far end of Paheli, into a mostly deserted area between two abandoned buildings. What she gestured to was a rusted, flickering fire escape ladder.

Ahmad eyed it dubiously. "That . . . doesn't look like it should be the entrance to some fancy palace."

Madame Nasirah shook her head. "You should know by now to not take anything in this world for granted."

Winnie gritted her teeth and grabbed the first rung. "Come on. Let's win this thing and go home."

Home.

Ahmad followed after her, wincing at every shake and shiver the ladder gave. Winnie vanished into the darkness above him. He looked back. Madame Nasirah gazed back up at him, as mysterious and hidden as she always was.

"Give my regards to the Architect," she called up, and then Ahmad was surrounded by clouds.

CHAPTER TWENTY-FOUR

AHMAD COULD FEEL THE cottony moisture closing about him while he flailed in confusion. How could there be clouds here?

"Ahmad, take my hand!" Winnie's voice was muffled, but close enough that he was able to reach out in its direction. He felt her fingers close around his hand. A moment later, he was yanked up and out of the fog, shaking his head to get the last of it out of his ears.

"What was . . ." he began, trailing off in amazement.

They hadn't only been in a cloud.

They were now standing on top of one, and not only that, in front of one of the most incredible palaces he had ever seen. It resembled the ones in the pictures from their trip to India, back when he had only been a small, pouty toddler: hundreds of eyelike windows and elegant domes.

It looked far too grand for one kid Architect, but then again, the Amari style was apparently overblown and oversized.

"This is incredible," Winnie whispered beside him.

"The Palace of Dreams," Ahmad responded. "I feel like . . . I've been here before."

Winnie squared her shoulders. "Good. Hold on to that feeling so we can get through this. Let's go."

They strode forward. They froze as the Palace of Dreams right split in two. A moment later, it split again.

The cloud-earth shook beneath them and they clung to each other, watching as palaces split and split and split to reveal more palaces, leaping out from the frame of one another like nesting dolls and fitting together with neat clicks before floating upward to dot the sky, resembling clouds of deceptively heavy brick and inlaid marble.

"I . . . wasn't expecting that," Ahmad managed as the last palace darted upward like a balloon with a cut string. "What are we supposed to do with that?"

"Maybe . . . nothing," Winnie said, staring upward

in amazement, as the palaces glided in place. "Maybe that was a show of force."

They continued forward, stopping within the grand main lobby. It resembled that of a museum, complete with walls lined with artwork and elegant glass cases filled with beautiful and bizarre antiques. But Ahmad and Winnie only had eyes for one.

"Doesn't that frame resemble the puzzle pieces?" Winnie asked. She kneeled down on the ground and started pulling the pieces out of the satchel, counting them carefully, and satisfied that they were all there.

Ahmad rushed off and lifted it off the wall. They squatted on the ground, trying to study the frame and how the pieces could click together.

"I think this is one of those puzzles that creates a box. The fame is probably the bottom," Winnie said finally. "The other pieces should click into place. Look, see how the joints are fashioned?" She traced her finger over one of the elegant blocks. Ahmad could see a raised line that looked like it might join with one of the others.

He nodded in agreement. "Okay, let's go."

He moved back, giving Winnie room to maneuver

the pieces as she saw fit. "The more I think about, the more I feel this is the type of world my aunt Zohra would thrive in," he remarked. "She used to have these things she messed around with on her hand all the time. They are called Turkish puzzle rings. There's this really morbid story behind them—"

But at the mention of the puzzle rings, the ground beneath them gave a sudden, violent tremor. "Um, what was that?" Winnie gasped.

"I'm not sure, but maybe the game is trying to tell us to hurry," Ahmad said.

Another piece slid neatly into place. "Almost there," Winnie said, her expression thoughtful, her tongue peeking out from between her lips. "Gosh, this Architect guy doesn't believe in easy wins, does he?"

"As flattering as the compliment is," a familiar voice broke in, sounding petulant and impatient, "that unfortunately isn't one of my projects. I suggest you put it down right now."

Ahmad and Winnie whirled around. There were the Architect and the MasterMind, both looking peevishly hot and a little more rumpled than usual.

"You again?" Winnie exclaimed. "Look, fair's fair.

We've followed your rules and done your weird challenges. We win!"

"You don't understand," the MasterMind burst out. "That box—"

"Holds the last challenge, we've got it." Winnie crossed her arms. "So you need to step aside and learn how to be a good sport."

Ahmad leaned in to slide the next piece in place. Faster than he would have expected, and surprising both him and Winnie, the Architect darted in and smacked it to the ground, nearly shattering all the work they'd accomplished.

"Hey! Lord Amari, that's going too far!"

"If you would both just listen, I wouldn't have to go that far." The Architect glared at Winnie when the girl reached for the piece. "Yes, you've completed the challenges—hooray for you, sorry but I didn't arrange for confetti in time. But now it's time to stop. Right now. You've done what I needed from you."

"Not until that box is finished, we haven't," Ahmad countered. "Look, isn't this what you wanted from us? This seems underhanded."

The MasterMind stepped forward. "Look, I'll handle this. That challenge you finished? That was the last challenge. You won. We're not happy about that, but we're willing to admit when we're beat."

Ahmad's brow furrowed. "But the Minaret—Madame Nasirah said she had a meeting with you and the challenge would be the last one."

It was the MasterMind's turn to look confused. "That annoying piece of errant code is still around? No. This—"

At a harsh look from Lord Amari, she clamped her lips shut. After a moment, she burst out again, "Look, we can't tell you why, but you—oh, you've finished it."

With a triumphant grin, Winnie held up the completed box high in her palm. Though the puzzle pieces and frame had been big and unwieldy, at Winnie's completion of the puzzle, the whole thing had shrunk down to a miniature version of itself.

"All in the wrist," she said deliberately, and winked at Ahmad. "How's that for using the art of distraction?"

"Nice job, Winnie!" Ahmad cried out in relief.

"No, no nice job!" the Architect snarled, stamping

his feet. He looked wild, his usually neat and slicked-back hair standing on end. His kurta was wrinkled beyond recognition. For a moment, Ahmad felt a twinge of unease. "Ahmad Mirza, listen here. You mustn't open that box. Do you hear me? I am the Architect and I am demanding that you don't open that box."

"Come on, Ahmad," Winnie said, inching backward with the box neatly balanced in her hand. "Let's go home."

Ahmad glanced between the two for a moment. Why was Lord Amari so desperate?

But Winnie beckoned. On the sweet, aromatic air, he could almost get a whiff of home: Ma's perfume, the warmth of it billowing about him as she pinched his cheeks and stuffed his mouth full of his favorite foods, and the spicy welcome of the kitchen, with his favorite masala chicken simmering on the stove.

"Let's go home," Ahmad said, stepping forward to join Winnie. Behind them, he could hear the MasterMind fall to her knees, hear the Architect roar, "Mirza, listen, please!"

But he focused on Winnie's bright smile and the promise of the world he wanted to return to.

And he lifted the lid.

Nothing happened.

"Wait," Winnie said, her brow furrowing. "What is—"

The Architect and the MasterMind were focused elsewhere, their gazes going right over Ahmad's and Winnie's heads.

"What is she doing here?" the MasterMind muttered. "The code should have uprooted her by now."

Ahmad and Winnie whirled around. There was Madame Nasirah, and for the first time, she had lifted her veil. She was smiling, her cheeks full and round, her lips pink and plump. But her teeth were sharp as knives. Not quite what Ahmad had expected.

"Well done, Ahmad and Winnie. You completed the challenge."

"What do you mean?" Ahmad demanded. "Nothing happened."

Winnie took a step back. "This doesn't feel good," she whispered. "But why?"

"And why are you speaking so casually of treason, Gamekeeper?" The Architect stepped forward, his voice a snarl. "Have you been dealing your own challenges to players in my name? Answer me!"

From within the very depths of the woman's form came an unholy chuckle. "You are one to talk of treason, aren't you, Amari?"

The Architect's face paled. "No. It can't be."

The box between Winnie's hands clattered to the ground and she gasped, backing away. The lid swung open and folds of utter blackness began to unfurl, like rich dark cloth, over the ground.

"Ironic, isn't it?" the voice that wasn't Madame Nasirah's continued. She began to grow large, towering over them. "One player toppled my world, and now another has restored it to me."

The MasterMind shrank away in terror, looking very much her age for once. Ahmad stared at the Architect.

"I warned you!" the other boy shrieked over the rising wind. "I warned you! Now you have him to reckon with!"

"Him?" Winnie echoed, her face growing pale, but Ahmad—watching as the ribbons of black began to curl over what was left of Madame Nasirah, the woman they thought was their friend—already knew who it was.

How could they have been so foolish?

How could they have let the fleeting promise of home allow them to willingly forget one of the key figures in Paheli? The one who created it to begin with?

"The monkeys were right. We forgot to keep an eye on every player," Ahmad croaked. "And now we have to reckon with him."

"I don't understand. Who is him?" Winnie demanded. "Why do you look so pale, Ahmad? What is going on?"

"The him he is speaking about," the voice came again, and this time it boomed all around them, as if the voice of space and time itself, "is me!"

There before them, floating in the air with a horrendous, leering grin, was the jinn, all clouds of black smoke billowing out of the shell of Madame Nasirah's skin. It had shed that skin like a butterfly flying out of its cocoon.

"Surprised?" the jinn crooned. It was bizarre and downright horrifying to hear that voice coming from behind Madame Nasirah's remaining shreds of cloth.

"I'm not," Winnie said firmly. "Something was wrong. I could feel it."

"Well, congratulations to you for having your wits about you. Now—" The jinn stretched out Madame Nasirah's disintegrating arms. "Time for you to see all that I really am."

CHAPTER TWENTY-FIVE

AHMAD'S HEART LODGED SOMEWHERE
beneath his throat—just beyond his esophagus,
just enough that his tongue felt smothered and
the words he tried to get out were suffocated. There
were prayers you could make, he knew, prayers of protection and deliverance. But he was frozen.

He hadn't expected this.

He knew about jinns. Since he was little, he had
been spoon-fed a lot of cautionary tales that happened
to some hypothetical brother, nephew, or cousin. And
always boiled down to it being their fault: "because he
didn't pray," "because he didn't listen to his mother," or
"because he talked too much about jinns where they
could hear."

From the downright impossible to the terrifyingly easy to swallow, there was a whole range of reasons to avoid the unseen world and what dwelled within it.

If you happened to see a jinn, you did not make deals with it.

You did not supplicate to it.

You did not trust it.

Ahmad could understand the distrust, staring at the jinn as it was now. It was muscled and carved in a way that suggested human physique, at least under the clanging sheets of armor and the helmet that drooped forbiddingly and shadowed its eyes, but the skin was reddish.

Once, Ahmad's father had told him about an early Muslim scholar who prayed to God so he could see the Devil. It was, as far as wishes went, a foolhardy one: the one you would hear a professor make in the opening moments of a horror movie. It was not a wish Ahmad would have made by any stretch of the imagination. But the scholar's request was heard. It was granted.

And he saw the Devil, in the hobbling, stooped visage of an old man, rushing eagerly up to him.

"But something about it made him shudder,"

Ahmad's baba had said in a hushed tone, as Ahmad clung to his sheets. "There was a way about the man's face, in his voice, the way he readily knew the scholar's name. There was an air about him. Tainted and malevolent. Evil. He did not want to get close to him. He kept his distance. The better for him."

"I just don't understand why God granted his wish to begin with," Ahmad had whispered.

"Sometimes you need to look evil in the eye to know why you avoid it."

Ahmad knew now. He shuddered, restless in his own skin, at the thought of the beings conjured from smokeless fire. But in the flesh, it was worse. Especially with Madame Nasirah's form curled up tight and lifeless as a cicada's shell next to its feet.

It leered at him. In spite of the shadow across its face, he could make out every one of its bright white teeth. Knife teeth.

And every one of them were curved and clenched.

"So," it rumbled. "Little Mirza. You've come this far. Even my dear"—it paused for a moment, and, the gruesome smile became ghastlier and more ripped about its edges—"nephew hasn't been able to stop your progress. No matter. You've done the job. And now, my Paheli returns to me!"

A great wind burst forth and the jinn swept out his—its—hand. Winnie and Ahmad grasped each other, and they could hear the confused cries of their former enemies.

"Uncle!" Lord Amari cried. "Uncle, ease up! I cannot stand!"

"You mewl and whimper like a kicked kitten when I have already been exposed to your plotting!" The jinn whirled on the Architect. Ahmad had been sure, up until now, that there was nothing that would make him feel sorry for spoiled, pampered, utterly heartless Amari.

Now he knew differently.

"You would have died in the cradle if it wasn't for my mercy," the jinn seethed. "Your father groveled on his knees and gave his very life so that you might be able to breathe. I taught you how to wield the game's finest tricks. I helped you lay pitfalls, stir up ancient bones, and enslave souls. What thanks did I get from you both? I was cast into a box and released only to see you trying to steal my world!"

The jinn's voice rose with every word until it was a roar.

The cowering Lord Amari scrambled backward on his hands, bumping into the MasterMind's knees. She made no effort to help him up.

"And here you lie, with more demands for my forgiveness—so like your mother, when she tried to escape my punishment. I took care of her. Now it is your turn. It is time for you to realize that you were at the mercy of my pleasure, rather than the other way around."

The MasterMind let out a slight whimper. The jinn turned to peer down at her.

"Ah yes, I nearly forgot the other conspirator. What did you intend to gain, my dear—riches greater than you could imagine or hold in your hands, or perhaps the satisfaction of a world laid out at your feet?"

Under his gaze, the MasterMind shrank.

"Hey!" Winnie stepped up, putting her hands on her hips. If she was nervous, she hardly showed it. Ahmad felt ashamed that his own knocking knees wouldn't let him join her. "Why don't you pick on someone your own size?"

"Ah," the jinn said. He threw his head back and

laughed. "Ironic that a human should tell me that. Your kind have gone up against mine throughout history, in spite of your size, in spite of your humble clay origins. Admirable, but foolish."

He turned to face the distant, glittering city, shaking his head in disgust. "My poor, darling Paheli—strung through with that horrid electricity and other cannibalistic enterprises. It is way past time for you to be purified."

He raised a hand, and in response, the Minaret let out a painful keen. Winnie winced. "Poor thing."

"You pity the ones that played with you?" The jinn raised an eyebrow in surprise. "Interesting, you humans. I thought you would thank me. I did give you that extra task to test your mettle. You pulled through better than I thought you would."

"Last task?" Winnie's eyes widened. "*You* were the one behind our goose chase? The fake challenge?"

"You're welcome," the jinn purred. "It was a chance for me to remind my city who truly owns it, after all. At least some of my servants didn't forget. Without that Titus Salt, I couldn't have engineered a level in time."

Winnie spluttered in shock.

Ahmad took advantage of the jinn's distraction to check on Lord Amari. "You okay, Amari?"

"Lord Amari to you." Amari gifted him with a look of distaste. "I've been better," he sniffed, but Ahmad could see the paleness of his cheeks, the tremors in his hands.

The MasterMind was keeping a safe distance, trembling from head to toe. Winnie gave her a look of disgust.

"So much for your partnership through thick and thin, huh?" Winnie spat. "Then again, I don't think villains are the type that stick up for each other."

The MasterMind bristled, pulling herself back up to her full height. "What do you know? It's been thick and thin since I came here!"

Suddenly she looked very, very young.

"I went from my parents being too busy to care, to being trapped in an entire world that wouldn't acknowledge me, but also expected to be saved. I saved it, when he couldn't. I made the code. I solved the problems. I kept us both alive!"

She roughly rubbed her nose against her sleeve and turned her back to them.

Winnie shook her head. "Okay, then, drama queen," she said, but her voice didn't have any bite to it.

She looked at Ahmad, her brow creased with worry while he examined the Architect for damages, keeping a wary eye on the jinn. The horrific creature was currently leering at Paheli, snapping his fingers and collapsing buildings, watching them crumble with a cackle.

"The best-laid of plans of mice and men," he snarled, "crumble in front of gods. Witness the return of your rightful master, my Paheli!"

The boy was battered and bruised, but with Ahmad's shadow falling on him, Amari roused up enough energy to contort his lips into a sneer.

"Goody Two-shoes," he seethed. "Such a Mirza!"

"What do you mean by that?" Ahmad asked.

"From my experience, people like you don't know when to give up and stop the encouraging speeches," the Architect replied. "You're living up to your name."

A minute ago, Ahmad would have stepped back and crossed his arms. Maybe he would let his sharp tongue get the best of him and blurt out something snarky. But now, he met the Architect's gaze steadily, extending his hand toward the other boy.

"Yes. I am a Mirza. Mirzas don't quit. I thought you didn't either."

The Architect looked at his hand for a long moment. Ahmad didn't move.

After a few minutes of the charged silence, the other boy grasped his hand and stood. Ahmad didn't turn his head, but he could feel Winnie smiling proudly at him and he pulled himself taller.

"Any ideas on what we should do?" Ahmad asked.

"I mean, it feels like our objective hasn't really changed," Winnie responded, eyeing the jinn's turned back tentatively. "We've just reached the Big Boss for the final battle. We finish the game, avenge Madame Nasirah, save our families and our world, and get out while the getting's good. The only problem is that I'm not sure how we beat a jinn without getting burned."

"Jinns are made of smokeless fire," Ahmad said automatically. "Not that I know whether or not that means he can burn us alive. It just—makes it feel less likely. But he's not going to let us out of here without a fight."

"If I might interrupt," the Architect's weak voice

came from behind them. "It seems our objectives are . . . quite similar."

"Well, that's a load of . . . manure," Winnie snorted, after a quick glance at Ahmad, who had to bite back a very inappropriate snort. "Your goal: Keep us in your game because you're a jerk and want friends but can't admit that because, well, you're a jerk. Our goal: Get out of the game after using you to wipe the floor because you're a jerk. I don't see any Venn diagram forming between those two."

"Your current goal is getting out of the game *alive*." The Architect raised his chin with indignance and, Ahmad was envious to see, only the slightest tremble. It was a skill he needed to work on himself. "Now, we share that goal. You heard what he—what he says he did to my mother. I'll be next."

He turned and spoke directly to Ahmad. "Mirzas are the best at games. At least, so I've learned from experience. And I think it's time for me to acknowledge that Amaris might need to learn from Mirzas in order to win too."

Ahmad couldn't believe what he was hearing. From

the raised eyebrows Winnie was giving the other boy, she couldn't either.

The MasterMind's jaw dropped. "If that isn't the most ridiculous—"

"I need you," Lord Amari said, holding Ahmad's gaze. "We *both* need you and Winnie in order to make it out of here. And for now, you need us, because Paheli lives within me. So why don't we combine our efforts and make it through together?"

CHAPTER TWENTY-SIX

AHMAD WAS TORN. WHAT Amari suggested actually did make sense. But how would they challenge the jinn? Could they really trust two probably not-quite-reformed villains?

Before anything else could be said or done, a tremor shook the earth.

Ahmad tumbled backward, Amari nearly toppling to the ground next to him.

"What was that?" demanded Winnie anxiously, but before any of them could respond, there was a soft cackle.

"That, my child," the jinn said, raising one reddish hand toward the sky, "was the sound of a new era!"

It was then that Ahmad realized the puzzle box was lying open again, its lid flapping in the wind.

And it was letting out a whole new challenge. Large letters flashed lightning swift against the darkening sky.

TRIAL: EVADE THE DEMON ARMY AND COMPLETE YOUR TASK—IF YOU CAN!

"D-demon army," Ahmad stammered.

But Winnie was already grasping his arm. "Ahmad! Look!"

Out of the box had popped a large green leg. Well, not only green. It was past that sickly, sallow shade, marked by mildew and aged rot. Wet black sludge dripped off its scaled knee and trickled over its clawed toes. What followed wasn't any more comforting: a torso held together by sheer might and stubborn sinew. Its head had one eye dangling onto a moth-bitten cheek and horrendously sized canines prodding from within bloodless lips.

"I did not sign up for zombie soldiers," Winnie said in a quavering voice. "Can we get them to bring the creepy birds back?"

Ahmad backed up a pace, keeping his grasp on Winnie.

The first hideous creature was joined by another. They multiplied as quickly as cells under a microscope.

"I—I don't think we get to be choosy anymore, Winnie."

"Indeed you don't," the jinn hissed. "You've been coddled and pampered enough by my nephew's sorry schemes and childish whims. It's time for a different game: a truly dangerous game that doesn't consider how you feel about it. What is it you young humans say? Ah, yes: The training wheels are off now!"

The jinn turned and gestured toward the closed, tight-lipped gate of Paheli. Before Ahmad's and Winnie's shocked eyes, it flung itself wide, pixels shimmering and quavering.

"The rules are simple. Whoever reaches that gate first . . . rules the world. Everybody wants to rule the world, don't they, young Mirza?"

"Isn't that a song?" Winnie mumbled under her breath.

"That sounds incredibly simple," scoffed the Architect, but his voice quavered.

The jinn sneered at him. "You would like to think so, wouldn't you, nephew?"

The Architect cowered, turning his gaze to the ground.

Ahmad narrowed his eyes. It did sound incredibly simple. Too simple to be true.

"I would try to negotiate, but I suppose that's off the table," he said as calmly as he could.

"You're a fast learner, Mirza," cooed the jinn. "Exactly the type of challenger I hoped you would be."

Ahmad looked back at Winnie, trying to read her expression. She nodded, just once.

We can do this.

We have to.

Ahmad turned back to the jinn, pulling his own spine taller. Winnie believed *they* could, together. The memory of the promise they made—to keep going, together— bolstered his courage.

"Game on."

CHAPTER TWENTY-SEVEN

THE JINN SPREAD ONE reddish hand and Ahmad
and Winnie startled back from a set of golden
stairs, nearly tumbling down them.

"Let's see how your memory works, shall we? Paheli
has often presented games featuring floating palaces,
and this will be another. Clamber up those stairs into
the palaces floating above. I will light up the doorways
in a certain pattern with chimes to guide you. If you
hear the chime after passing through a doorway—well,
then, you are on the right track. But if you pass through
at least three doors that are not correct—"

The jinn chuckled and Ahmad clutched his own
arms out of fear that the skin would squirm right off. It
was a disgusting sound. "Well, let us just say that there

won't be that much of you to clean up off the sand."

"Ew," Winnie said softly.

Ahmad swallowed hard. "And . . . and if we make it through the right doors?"

"You proceed to the next palace and the palace after that. Your goal is this."

The jinn closed his fingers. When they opened, a small flame burned within them. "This . . . is my heart. Well, you would call it that. I wager my life with yours. That should keep it interesting for all of us."

The jinn smirked at the two of them and snapped his fingers. The flame vanished into a carved monkey figurine. It chittered at them, skittering upward off the jinn's hand and into the sky.

"Where did it go?" Winnie gasped.

"Follow the right pathway, and you'll see," the jinn responded. "Now then, on your marks . . ."

"We'll split up," whispered the Architect harshly. "Teams of two. If we find it first—"

"Could we even trust you with finding it first? And don't tell us what to do," Winnie hissed back. "Ahmad and I are doing our own thing. You do whatever you want but don't get in our way and don't mess things up."

"*Get set . . .*"

Ahmad and the MasterMind rolled their eyes at each other. "For now," the MasterMind said, "let's agree to not get along, but at least try to keep each other alive. Fair?"

"Fine."

"Go!" the jinn roared. Ahmad and Winnie scrambled for the stairs.

"Oh, I hate this," Winnie hummed nervously. "I can see the ground. . . ."

"Keep looking up and focus on the game!" Ahmad panted. "Remember how you flew that car? You could see the ground then, too."

"That was different!"

They cleared the last step. Ahmad made the mistake of turning around and looking to see where the MasterMind and the Architect were: several flights of uneven stairs below. Winnie was right. You could see beneath every rung. The entire world of the game sparked and shimmered beneath them, pixelated and glorious, and a suggestion of the familiar sprawl of New York City somewhere beneath it—but also very, very far away from where they were now.

"Keep looking up and focus on the game," Winnie repeated, nudging him in the side. "First palace. Let's go."

They rushed through the door, hearing the soft chime. They were inside an opulent courtyard that reminded Ahmad, oddly enough, of the inside of a bird's nest: hundreds and thousands of tiny windows were set in the walls, letting in light that shimmered. Before them was a large wall of glorious gemstones slick with tumbling water, tossing bright panes of light everywhere it could.

"It's beautiful," Winnie gasped.

Ahmad caught sight of what was ahead. He groaned aloud. "Oh man, really?"

There were hundreds of doors.

"How are we going to do this?" Winnie whimpered.

Ahmad grasped her hand. "Wait."

They paused and strained their ears. There was a familiar scratching in the walls.

"The mice!" Winnie gasped. "But how——"

"No time for those questions! Quick!" Ahmad gasped. They lunged through the first doorway, only half aware of the giddy chimes that followed in their wake. "We need . . . to listen for them! It's our only chance."

They barreled through the palace, up an elegant curved spine of a stairwell, and fumbled through piles of languidly placed cushions. Within minutes they had cleared it and were halfway through the next.

"The noise is fading!" Winnie called out behind Ahmad. "How are we going to be able to tell now?"

Ahmad gritted his teeth and kept hurdling forward, but he knew she was right. They wouldn't be able to make it through every palace in time. On top of that, they also had to keep an eye out for the little monkey. He stopped short as he spotted a bird, hovering right in a doorframe as the light dimmed out from the wood structure beneath it.

"Ugh, that was the last one," Winnie groaned, catching her breath. She glanced over Ahmad's head, squealed, and backed up. "Oh, no, no, no. Not again!"

"Wait, Winnie. I think it's here to help us!"

The bird stared down at the two of them for a minute. And then, it elegantly unfurled its wings and glided off through the doorway.

"Are you sure, Ahmad? Paheli does what it can to

survive, remember? We could be falling into a trap with this."

"We have to trust that Paheli wants us to win as much as we want to win," Ahmad said firmly.

There was a chirrup over their head. The bird was circling, waiting impatiently for them to follow.

"Lead the way!" Ahmad called out, and it flew back out the door.

They followed, skittering over elegant rugs and barely avoiding collisions with stone statues. They cleared another door, and another. Another palace flew out from beneath their feet, and another.

"Start looking out for the monkey!" Winnie gasped in Ahmad's ear. "I feel like we're halfway through the palaces and I haven't seen hide nor hair of it."

But when they landed in the next palace, they stopped short. There were the Architect and the MasterMind, out of breath and red-faced, teetering back and forth on top of a large bookcase.

"Look out!"

The Architect called out and Winnie dragged Ahmad back out the doorway. The chime sounded again, high and sweet, and they just barely heard the crash and clatter of books falling on the floor. Ahmad and Winnie peeked their head back in.

The bird perched sulkily on the bust of a tiger's head—bizarrely human in its whimsical expression and elegantly perched silk turban—and the MasterMind and the Architect rubbed their heads in the midst of a pile of books.

"How did you get here so fast?" Winnie demanded.

The Architect managed to look smug from his askew position on the floor. "This game is mine, you know."

"Funny, could've fooled me when your 'uncle' tossed you to the side and took over."

A fight was obviously about to start, so Ahmad hastily stepped in. "So what are you trying to do? I don't think we have time for amateur rock-climbing practice."

"If you must know," the MasterMind broke in snottily, "we saw that infernal monkey in here. I was trying to see if I could find the room's source code and locate its root into my interface and maybe . . . scramble a few things up to make it harder for the creature to hide itself, but that didn't go so well."

Ahmad peeked out the nearest window. The ground was nauseatingly far below them, and he could just make out a glimpse of the jinn's broad shoulders and his moving hands. . . . What was he doing? Ahmad squinted to try and make it out.

"Well, I think we need to go faster. The jinn is making more of his ghoulish minions and it seems like they are coming after us!"

"Not to add more to worry about, but you guys do realize the connection to the other palaces cuts off our own escape route?" the MasterMind said, glancing between Ahmad and Winnie. "We'll have to work fast and with the awareness that we have nowhere else to go when they *do* catch up to us."

Ahmad and Winnie exchanged glances. "That just gives us more incentive," Ahmad said. He and Winnie lunged up the staircase.

"So where do you even want to begin to look?" Winnie panted. "This isn't going to be easy."

Ahmad had a weird feeling in his gut. Something made him feel like the monkey would pick somewhere obvious rather than really hiding itself. After all, hadn't the last monkey tried to help them? And in spite of being a jinn's heart, couldn't this monkey maybe change its role at the thought of its world being taken apart and scrambled? But maybe he was overthinking things again.

Ahmad threw open the balcony door and froze. There, leaning over the railing and crooning to itself, was the monkey.

"All right," Ahmad whispered. "Easy does it."

He inched forward. Ahmad was never the best at handling delicate operations, whether they were the type that you had to show your work for on a math test, or just navigating the ins and outs of the school day.

But now, he had to try. For his parents, for Winnie's parents, for Winnie, and . . . for himself. No matter what his teachers thought, no matter the bad days he had, he was a Mirza. He could do it.

If he could just inch forward more . . .

Ahmad snagged the monkey's tail. It let out an ear-piercing shriek. Below them, the jinn swiveled his head upward, his eyes widening as he caught sight of what Ahmad had in his hands.

"Now, hold still," Ahmad grunted, squeezing the

monkey about the stomach. "This hurts me too, I . . . promise!"

"Stop right there," the jinn snarled. Another squeeze, and the monkey choked. Something skittered over the tiles. Winnie appeared at the door, her eyes wide.

"Winnie!" Ahmad hollered. "Quick!"

They heard a shriek below them and an eerie moan. The demon army had managed to break into the palace and the Architect and MasterMind were trapped. There was no time to hesitate.

"Ahmad!" a voice called from outside. Ahmad turned, and his stomach unclenched with relief.

"Vijay Bhai!"

Vijay Bhai was leaning out of the basket of a beautiful hot air balloon. It seemed to be some sort of hybrid of the old Paheli style and the MasterMind's new neon inventions. It had an old-fashioned wicker basket, but a beautiful bloom of a balloon attached, like something right out of Times Square, flashing brightly through different colors like the fabric was cut from an actual rainbow.

"Ahmad!" Vijay Bhai called. "Jump!"

Ahmad skittered toward whatever had fallen out onto the floor. He rushed to the balcony and tossed himself out, but not before calling out over his shoulder, "Winnie! Next room!"

"Got it!" she called back, and disappeared.

For a moment, as Ahmad dived, he felt the sickening lurch of his stomach and gravity pulling his body downward, falling, falling, falling. This was it. This was the end.

But then, the balloon swooped below him, and Vijay Bhai dragged him into the basket, moments before the jinn's huge fist took off the balcony where he had been standing.

"Yikes," Ahmad exhaled. "Thanks, Vijay Bhai!"

"Don't thank me yet," Vijay Bhai said, his eyes magnified behind a pair of what appeared to be digitized goggles. Numbers scrolled over the lenses. "Brace yourself! He's going to aim for us now!"

Vijay Bhai jerked, and the entire balloon careened to the side, narrowly avoiding red-tinged fingers.

"Stop right there, balloon boy," the jinn seethed beneath them. "You can't keep this up forever."

"Try me!" Vijay Bhai hollered back. He turned to

Ahmad. "I'm going to get you as close to that window as you can. Put all your energy into your feet and try to imagine you're a spring. Jump and don't look down."

Ahmad swallowed hard and nodded.

The balloon swerved and slid closer to the window.

"You're making me lose my temper, little Mirza," the jinn rasped. Ahmad focused on his uncle's eyes.

"You can do this," Vijay Bhai said firmly. "You're a Mirza."

Ahmad jumped. He did look down, but all he caught sight of was his own blurry sneakers.

"Oof!" He landed hard, every bone in his body shrieking. But there was no time to worry about that.

"Ahmad!" Winnie gasped, rushing up to him. "Are you okay? You still have the soul?"

"Yeah," Ahmad managed. He drew the monkey figurine out of his pocket.

"Don't you dare!" the jinn roared. Ahmad could feel the palace jittering beneath them. "You . . . foolish . . . impudent . . . human!"

Winnie set her jaw, backing up toward the door. She held up a hand. Ahmad tossed forward the flame and her fingers clamped around it.

The jinn's giant head appeared at level with the balcony, peering at them triumphantly. Ahmad backed away, eyes wide. The creature was ablaze from its head to its toes, fire dancing up and down its arms.

"You shall not . . . overtake me that easily," the jinn panted, reaching out for him with a blazing arm. "I know about you, Ahmad Mirza. This won't save you from who you are, and what you are. This is a battle you can't win, and you're waging it alone."

"No," Ahmad said. "No, I'm not alone. And this a battle we're winning. Together."

The jinn caught sight of Winnie behind Ahmad, though, and wailed.

"No!"

Winnie stamped on the flame with one foot. It extinguished against the cool marble tiles.

Everything happened very quickly after that, but Ahmad couldn't say exactly what happened.

The jinn keened and Ahmad heard a sudden, vicious sound: a catching of flame and a collapsing in all at once that reminded him of a house on fire crumbling apart.

The palace itself fell too. Ahmad and Winnie clung

to each other, screaming, as it plummeted and crashed against the ground around them.

They were tossed up and back down, groaning as elbows and stomachs collided.

"Winnie, you okay?" Ahmad gritted out.

"Ugh, I think every bone is broken. Oh, wait, maybe not my pinkie."

"We did it," Ahmad whispered. "We did it!"

Winnie scrambled up, her eyes wide. "Did we? We need to go outside and see!"

Ahmad stumbled up and the kids rushed out. Could that really have been the end of the jinn?

CHAPTER TWENTY-EIGHT

AHMAD AND WINNIE PICKED their way out of the rubble into the sunlight.

About them were the mangled remains of a hundred beautiful palaces. "Poor things," Winnie whimpered, leaning down to touch one shattered tile. "I'm so sorry!"

"Poor palaces? What about us?" Lord Amari's disgruntled voice called from what seemed a distance.

Ahmad was surprised to find a relieved smile tugging at his lips.

He fought it away and turned around to retort, "You guys make it through every time. Unfortunately."

The MasterMind smirked back, looking no worse for wear in spite of the sand clinging to her hat, but the Architect groaned from behind her. "What do you mean, 'unfortunately'? Don't make me regret sparing your life."

"Yeah, yeah," Winnie groused. "Look, just be grateful we made it out alive and your so-called uncle didn't . . . wait." Her eyes widened and her hand flew to her mouth. "Um, Ahmad. Did we kill a jinn?"

Before Ahmad could answer, the MasterMind broke in cheerily. "Sure did."

She kicked at what Ahmad now saw was a large scorch mark on the ground.

"Probably have the whole lot of his tribe plotting revenge as we speak," the Architect added grimly. "Jinns are not the most . . . reasonable creatures."

Winnie groaned. "Great. Just what I need."

"But what about Madame Nasirah?" Ahmad broke in anxiously.

The Architect crossed his arms. "Don't think I don't take care of my own Gamekeeper. She'll be back in her shop where she belongs, probably toddling along and crooning to her beloved teapots without any aware- ness of what happened."

The MasterMind rolled her eyes. "He didn't like

my suggestion that we replace her with a bot."

Ahmad sighed in relief—and then gasped as the ground shook beneath him.

"What was that?"

The MasterMind's smile melted away and she looked grim. "That is our final timer. Paheli is eating away at itself. The jinn that kept it alive . . . well, we just established what happened to him. You freed Paheli but sealed its fate."

"We need to get out!" Winnie gasped out, grasping Ahmad's arm.

"Way ahead of you there," the MasterMind responded, stepping back to reveal a glimmering doorway. Through it, Ahmad could make out the suggestion of skyscrapers, milling tourists on distant black asphalt, and the beautiful green expanse of Central Park.

New York City. *Home.*

It was that close now.

"You both need to go through," the Architect said firmly. "We have minutes to spare."

"You don't have to tell me twice," Winnie said fervently, but Ahmad anxiously asked, "Wait, you guys aren't coming too?"

The Architect opened his mouth, but the MasterMind jammed her elbow between his ribs. "Ow! . . . Well, after much discussion, we decided that staying here was the best solution," he said grimly. "This . . . this is my world after all, the only world I've ever known. I will go down with the ship."

"What he should say," the MasterMind snapped, "is that his partner is a genius at coding. I'll get this ship back up and running. Don't be so gloomy." She rubbed her arm, and added quietly, "It's not like I have anywhere else to go anyway."

The Architect, too, looked away for a long minute. "And I . . . I want to know what happened to my mother. Where she is in here. What the jinn said, about getting rid of her . . . I've been scared. If she's in here, somewhere, at least I can see her one more time."

"And you're just going to let us go?" Winnie narrowed her eyes at both of them. "When you know you're staying here and might die?"

But Ahmad understood. Paheli was something that was part of his world, but not in the same way it was for Lord Amari. It was his whole world.

Instead he said softly, "This is your chance, you

know. To make Paheli different this time. To let go of the game."

Lord Amari looked at him, saying nothing.

"You can't—" Winnie started again.

"Don't make us regret letting you go," the MasterMind snapped back. "Just go home and count your lucky stars you made it out in time. You have two minutes left."

"Thank you," Ahmad said. It didn't even surprise him now that he meant it. "I hope you guys survive this. I hope Paheli is able to live for itself now."

"Just get going," the Architect said, but both of them looked surprisingly touched.

Ahmad turned, and then his eyes widened.

"But . . . Vijay Bhai! Where is he?"

"Look out below!" a voice called cheerfully from above.

Winnie looked up, gasped, and shoved Ahmad aside.

"Move! Quick!"

Moments later, a lanky body tumbled down, hitting the sand with a painful sounding "oomph." The MasterMind winced delicately.

"Nice job," the Architect said sarcastically.

"I'm okay," Vijay Bhai said, muffled by the sand. He sat up slowly and brushed himself off, grinning at his nephew.

"Like I would let you go home without me."

"Your loyalty to Paheli is admirable," the Architect said, and then cowered as Vijay Bhai slowly rose to his feet. He stared down at the spoiled boy with distaste.

"I wish I could say you've grown, but you obviously haven't."

Winnie let out a nervous-sounding giggle. "Ouch," she whispered to Ahmad.

"Yes, well," the Architect blustered, trying to pull himself up higher. "Be glad that you aren't feeling my wrath and—"

The MasterMind elbowed him in the ribs again. "Just get going," she said to the trio as they dusted themselves off again. "Before he really picks up steam."

Ahmad grasped Winnie's hand. They glanced back at Paheli one more time. They could see the seamed exterior of the Minaret now as it teetered back and forth. It snapped in half, revealing an ancient inner core: tall marble and a green flash of fire at the top.

"Good-bye, dream city," Ahmad said softly.

He and Winnie stepped through the doorway, and onto the sticky grass of Central Park. They turned to see the Architect and MasterMind walking toward the depths of Paheli.

They could hardly make out anything but their small bodies moving against the sand. The entire portal shimmered out of existence. There was nothing there except for a brick wall. But Ahmad and Winnie only had eyes for the park exit and the street beyond it. They rushed farther into it, staring eagerly at what lay ahead. In front of them was one of the most beautiful scenes they had ever laid their eyes on: their neighborhood of the Upper East Side, with not a grain of sand to be seen on its worn but welcoming pavements, not an unhappy face turned upward to the sky as kids skipped home from after-school classes, and tourists milled toward waiting taxis with shopping bags in hand.

"Home," Ahmad sighed happily. "It's perfect."

"Do you think Paheli is gone?" Winnie said anxiously.

Vijai Bhai turned to stare back at where the door

had been, the kids following his gaze. Every trace of it had disappeared.

Ahmad thought for a moment about the look in Lord Amari's eyes, about Madame Nasirah's warm smile and ready teapot, and the beautiful streets he wished he could have walked peacefully.

"I hope not," he said quietly. "But I think that was the end of it for us."

Within minutes, the three of them had reached Ahmad's building, and the once too-fast elevators seemed tame after their rickshaw racing and other adventures.

Ma opened the front door with a smile, the smell of spicy chicken curry and freshly steamed rice wafting out behind her.

"Ahmad! Goodness, I thought you would have started your project by now. Mr. Willis said you left an hour ago! Is this your friend Winnie?"

Ma wiped her hand on the dish towel tucked in at her waist. "Winnie's father said he would be back in two hours, and . . . oh, what's the matter?"

Ahmad buried his head into her orna and snuggled himself tightly. He could practically feel the silly grin radiating off Winnie's face, but he focused on soaking in his mother's scent and feel and everything that just made her his mom, whole and warm and definitely not frozen—though there was a suspicious dampness at the ends of her scarf.

"Oh, Ahmad," Ma said, squeezing him back. "You sweetheart. Come on, baby, set the table."

"All right, all right," Ahmad said as Baba, on the couch, waved at him with a smile, his cell phone still pressed against his ear. Ma turned back toward the kitchen and then stopped, whirling around to face the third person in the room.

"Vijay? I thought you went out for a walk."

Vijay Bhai froze, his eyes wide.

"Oh, um . . . I did," he blustered, "but it looked like it was going to rain."

Ma stared out the sunlit window pointedly, and then at her childhood friend.

"Okay, then," she said, with a shrug. "Ahmad, the table?" She grinned. "And a plate for Vijay Bhai, too."

Ahmad started for the china cabinet and then froze.

"Ahmad? What is it?" Winnie demanded. When she reached him, she stopped short. There was a mouse beneath the cabinet, blinking up at them. Its cheeks were suspiciously round, and in its paws . . . was that one of Ahmad's precious chenna murki?

Ahmad started forward and it squeaked, skittering toward the ajar front door and out into the hallway.

"It couldn't be—" Winnie started. Ahmad firmly shook his head. "No. We were supposed to be the only ones who could make it through."

They looked after the mouse for a moment. Ahmad cleared his throat. "So. Um. About earlier, with the package and the project—"

He yelped as Winnie's elbow neatly found its way between his ribs. Apparently, she'd learned plenty from the MasterMind. "Let's not start with the formality. We lived through a vicious board game together. Let's stuff our faces and congratulate ourselves on a job well done, and talk about our project. Together."

"Okay." Ahmad felt a big, goofy grin breaking out. He couldn't control it. *Together.* Apparently, they hadn't left that word back in Paheli.

"Okay. Let's set the table so we can figure out how to make this as epic as possible."

They walked into the dining room together. And,

as Winnie pulled faces when Ahmad set a plate down too hard, and Ma bustled past with platters of food, it felt very much like this was the beginning of a new adventure.

Maybe the beginning of a beautiful friendship, too.

Even Ahmad Mirza, it seemed, could have one.

ACKNOWLEDGMENTS

As always, I begin by thanking God for allowing me to pursue what often felt like an unattainable dream. Every development in this publishing journey has been unexpected and wondrous in ways I could never have arranged or hoped for on my own. I am so, so grateful.

Thank you to my family: my father for his unwavering enthusiasm for the process; my mother for being a supportive first reader and always asking the question, "Does this feel good to you?"; and my sister Sumayyah and brother Sahnoon for, as always, being both delightful and irksome at the same time.

I thank the family members who are no longer here but whose legacies have grounded me: my grandfathers—one for his strength and his name, which I use in his honor, and the other for his love and confidence in me from when I was very young, which I hold on to when I remember that he isn't here to see this—my uncles, and my paternal grandmother, my Dadi Apa, who greeted the news of my debut with pride and I know would have been happy to hold this book in her hands as well.

I infinitely thank my grandma for being a constant presence of encouragement and chocolate throughout my childhood and now. Thank you as well to my uncles and aunts, and my cousins, for the sweets and celebration every time I have good news to share (and a special thank you to my big sister-cousin Riya Apu for being an instant cheerleader and book pusher as soon as she heard the news). I would be remiss if I didn't particularly thank my biggest fan and sweet baby sister, my dear cousin Nusaybah Mohsini, who believes in me even on the rough drafting days when I can't believe in myself. She, my cousin Ashlie Watson, and Farha Ferdous played a huge part in shaping Farah and her family into people, and not merely characters, and I appreciate and love all of them for it. (Thank you to my baby cousin Farhan, as well, for being a reference when I thought, "What would Ahmad do?")

Thank you to Sona Charaipotra and Dhonielle Clayton for folding me into Cake Literary with love and patience, from when I was an intern to now. You both inspire me to be a better writer and a better person. Thank you to Victoria Marini for being an incredible agent on behalf of Cake Literary, being an epic cheerleader, and dealing with the red tape with grace and care.

Words cannot express how much Zareen Jaffery means to me, as an inspiration and an editor. Thank you for your kindness and for extending your belief in me to a second book. This industry would not be the same without you and your efforts, and I cannot wait to see how Salaam Reads continues to grow and the wonderful stories it produces in the years to come. Thank you as well to the wonderful Justin Chanda, the hard-working Lisa Moraleda and everyone on the team at S&S.

Thank you to Shveta Thakrar, Ronni Davis, Shan Chakraborty, Katherine Locke and Nita Tyndall for all the pep talks and stardust when I needed it most, and Wendy Xu for being the best petty auntie friend a girl could ask for. I would not be the writer I am without the support and love of my Iron Keys, Natasha Heck (a.k.a. the Commander) and Amparo Ortiz (a.k.a. Dragon Tamer).

I could not have gotten through this book without my unnis—Kat Cho (the nice one), Nafiza Azad (the tough love one) and Axie Oh (the CP and support from the very beginning one). I love you guys and I hope you always know it. Our group chat still remains the best group chat, hands down. So much love to my other sisters: Nicole (heart), Aeman (big) and Fati (salt), who are willing to talk about everything and nothing.

Thank you to the best reference librarian in the world, Ms. Kiersten, who has been guiding me to good reads and dispensing excellent advice since I was two years old.

I would like to thank my 2017–18 seventh-, eighth-, and ninth-grade ELA classes at MDQ Academy, for being such great kids and excellent students, and getting me through a rough year with laughs and hugs and plenty of good reads. You were the best kids a first-year teacher could ask for and I will never forget it.

(My seventh graders—Alina, Amir, Hayaa, Asiye, Ayoub, Sumaya, Shiza, Hasan, Maryum, Ayesha A., Hamid, Mohid, Maryam A., Mohammad, Ayesha I., Marium F., Yassna, Elijah, Murtuza, Aleena A., Aleena S., Usman, Furghub, Nabila, and Ameen—made me promise as their homeroom teacher to acknowledge them in my next book. I told you guys I would!)

A special thank you as well for their sweetness and encouragement to Amar of last year's eighth grade, Aaliyah of last year's tenth grade, and Sabrena of last year's eleventh grade, who are all awesome readers and writers and will do great things in this world.

Thank you to my dearest friend Moira Fox-Maranski for keeping it real since September 2006 when we were both teen dorks holding intense discussions in between the library shelves and keeping a weather eye out for our baby brothers to interrupt. I love you and appreciate you more than words can say.

A special thank you to the author-heroes who took me under their wing and let me soak in their wisdom: among others, my middle grade fairy godmother Anne Ursu, Aisha Saeed,

Sabaa Tahir, Libba Bray, Ellen Oh, and Tracey Baptiste. It is always an honor.

I wish I could name all the lovelies of my Twitter feed and online publishing haunts by name. The support through the particularly dark nights, the tagging in pictures of Sailor Mercury and encouraging words during writing sprints mean everything. You guys are everything. Thank you forever for being my community.

And thank you, once again, to you, dear reader. Thank you for the love and encouragement. Thank you for the bought, borrowed, or bartered copies, the bookmarks, and the dog-ears. Thank you for the giddy selfies taken in signing lines, and the excited whispers of your favorite scenes. May you always have good friends at your side, hope in your heart, and the winning hand in your favorite game. You deserve it.

A Reading Group Guide to *The Gauntlet* and *The Battle* by Karuna Riazi

About the Books

Farah Mirza and her friends, Essie and Alex, are determined to rescue Farah's little brother, Ahmad, who has been lured inside a game called Paheli. As the boundaries between reality and fantasy fade and the friends become trapped themselves, they are isolated from the world they know in New York City. A quest for survival drives them to challenge the power and authority of the Architect in a mission to dismantle the city itself. When the time comes to challenge the game a second time, Ahmad is now twelve, confronting Paheli's riddles with his friend Winnie. They enter a newly coded world, rebuilt by the MasterMind with computer-programmed upgrades controlled by the Architect. Underneath it all, the city is rotting with dread and desperation, powered by corruption and greed. As power struggles develop, alliances form, and surreal quests and challenges unfold with strange and supernatural creatures. Winning depends on the children's ability to face and overcome injustice with the courage to speak up for what they believe in, working together to find their way back home.

Discussion Questions

1. *The Gauntlet* and The *Battle* are narratives told from two different points of view. Farah's first-person narrative creates the tone of *The Gauntlet*. Did you relate to her voice? How does her perspective impact the way the story is told?

2. A third-person omniscient narrator sets the tone for *The Battle*. Did switching points of view affect the way you experienced these stories? If so, in what ways? Why do you think the author chose a third-person narrator to tell the story of *The Battle*?

3. What drives each of the children to enter the game and willingly put themselves in danger? Consider Farah, Essie, Alex, Ahmad, and Winnie. What do their convictions reveal about them? Would you

have followed them into the game? Explain your answer.

4. The children face multiple fears in their dedication to a purpose greater than themselves. As Vijay Bhai forewarned Ahmad, "'You can't win this game unless you take chances.'" Discuss some of these fears the children encountered and found the courage to confront. What were the outcomes? Describe a time in your life that required courage, and how you handled the situation. What did you learn from the experience?

5. The author explores a variety of themes including loss, loneliness, isolation, helplessness, social confusion, identity, bullying, injustice, belonging, vulnerability, resilience, respect, compassion, courage, hope, and friendship. Find examples of some of these in the book. What roles do these themes play in the games? What roles do they play in your life? What makes you feel safe, protected, and valued? Explain your answers.

6. How do the children feel about trust? How responsible are they for each other's well-being and actions? How important is trust to you? How responsible

do you think we should be for one another?

7. The children could not have survived the games without the help of others. What supernatural companions do they have to guide them? Consider T. T. and Henrietta especially. What are their roles? Why are these new friends so willing to help the children through the challenges?

8. Pace and momentum affect the telling of these stories. Constant commotion, upheavals, confrontations, and confusion contribute to a chaotic narrative that creates tension, fear, and uncertainty, keeping the children—and the reader—off-balance. What scene did you find most suspenseful? What was the most critical choice that had to be made, and what was the outcome? What would you have done?

9. Aunt Zohra has a "long-forgotten trauma and haunted past." How does her experience in the game affect her behavior in the present? Why does she keep her involvement in the game a secret?

10. What is Vijay Bhai's role in both stories? Describe the relationship he has with the other characters.

What do you think of him and his intentions? Explain your answers.

11. In your opinion, what is Farah's greatest strength? What are Ahmad's, Winnie's, Essie's, Alex's, and Vijay Bhai's? In what ways are these strengths crucial to the unfolding stories?

12. Which character do you relate to most? What is it about that character that you identified or connected with? Which character is most unlike you, and for what reasons? How would you go about getting to know them better or finding something about them you can relate to? Who would you most want to be like? Explain your answer.

13. Why do the Architect and the MasterMind destroy the dream district of Lailat, called "a place of eternal night and endless carnivals"? What does this reveal about their motivations?

14. What were your initial impressions of Ahmad in *The Gauntlet*? Did your thoughts and feelings about him change as you read *The Battle*? In what ways?

15. Winnie often notices things that Ahmad does not. She has little patience for pretense and is not easily fooled. Are her suspicions about Madame

Nasirah justified? Give examples from the text that arouse her suspicion. What do you think of Madame Nasirah?

16. In order to fully understand the loyalties in Paheli and the complexities of the games, it's important to consider other viewpoints. What are the Architect's, the MasterMind's, Titus Salt's, and the jinn's backstories? What is the significance of their motivations? Find examples that give the reader deeper insight into each of these characters and their personal goals and struggles. Who or what is the true power in Paheli? Who are the true heroes?

17. Which parts of the story most held your interest? What scenes were the most surprising, confusing, compassionate, or memorable to you? Explain your answers.

18. What do you think is the core message of these two stories? What effect did they have on you? Have they changed your perspective about anything? Will you think about certain people or situations differently in the future?

19. Which moments of the children's journey were most relatable? Which parts inspired you? Do you

see yourself differently after reading these stories?

20. Did you find the ending of *The Battle* satisfying? Explain your reasoning. Do you feel there are things left unresolved or uncertain?

21. What do you think life in New York City will be like for the children after experiencing the challenges in the city of Paheli? What new realizations and inner strengths might they bring home with them?

Extension Activities

1. Do parts of Karuna Riazi's stories remind you of other books or movies? How do these similarities strengthen your understanding and enjoyment of her stories? Discuss some references that stand out for you, what they call to mind, and how they enhance aspects of *The Gauntlet* and *The Battle*.

2. Write a letter to one of the characters in either *The Gauntlet* or *The Battle*. Who would you choose? What would you want him or her to know? What encouragement would you give? What questions would you ask? What would you reveal about yourself?

3. Ahmad struggles with Attention Deficit Hyperactivity Disorder (ADHD) and believes himself to be lacking in several fundamental ways. He says that he "trusted Winnie but he couldn't quite trust himself the same way." What do you think he means by that? In what ways is he challenged by his disorder? In what ways does his ADHD serve him well as he maneuvers through the dangers and chaos? Learn about possible symptoms of ADHD and relate them to the life Ahmad is living.

4. Winnie suggests, "Don't accept the label they put on you." To what extent do labels define us? Discuss ways in which you label yourself, and ways in which you and your friends label one another. What are the results of doing this? Brainstorm as a class ways in which you can educate, prevent, or speak out against prejudices and sterotypes.

5. The Middle Eastern setting is essential to the story, and the experiences are rich with visually descriptive imagery and strong characterization that suggest potential for a screenplay. Visualize the special effects needed. Imagine whom you would cast in the lead roles. How would you represent the chaos

from one precarious and unpredictable moment to the next? Discuss your ideas with a partner.

6. The author creates mental images using vivid and clear descriptions. Choose a moment from either of the two novels, and describe what you felt as you read the passage, responding in a way that reflects the experience for you. Your response can be in the form of a painting, collage, musical composition, poem, dance, or any other form of expression that is meaningful to you. Share your creation with your peers.

7. Author Karuna Riazi includes an abundance of references to the food, clothing, and architecture of Muslim culture. In a small group, research the references that most interest you, and share your findings.

The Gauntlet: Lexile ® HL700L

The Battle: Lexile ® 710L

The Lexile reading level has been certified by the Lexile developer, MetaMetrics®

This guide was prepared in 2019 by Judith Clifton, Educational Consultant, Chatham, MA. Visit

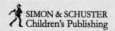

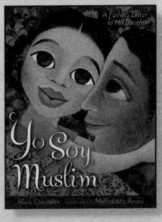

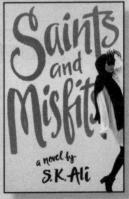

Once invited, you must take care, lest you vanish between the here and there. Welcome to the

Hotel Between.

"Magic and mystery draw you into *The Hotel Between*,
and I couldn't leave until I knew all its secrets.
Can I make a reservation yet?"

—JAMES RILEY,
New York Times bestselling author of the Story Thieves series

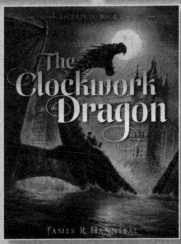

Effie Truelove believes in magic, but will that be enough to save the world?

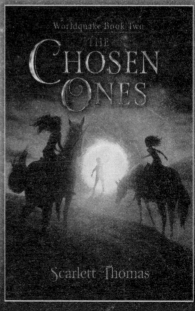